The Secret Club
The Power Club Book Two

Greg Gildersleeve

Dedication

No writer is an island. He or she is a universe of family and friends, acquaintances and passersby, and the occasional animal or two. So many people contributed in large and small ways to this book, whether they knew it or not.

Special shout-out to the former Monday Night Writers Group for critiquing early drafts of this story...to the gang at Drawing Frenzy for allowing me to express other sides of my creativity...to Wordwraiths Write Night for the friendship and inspiration...and to Stephanie Hansen, my agent, for opening doors I never knew existed.

To the memory of Tim H., who was to me what Kyle was to Damon.

Prologue

He's gaining on me.

A rift opened in Jayden's netherfield. Dodging it was easy, but next time he might not be so lucky. The "netherfield" was his name for the world inside the telephone wires—electronic impulses shooting backwards and forwards across an endless spaghetti of cables. Only Jayden could visit this world and travel in it. It was his secret place—until the rifts opened.

He didn't know how the other boy kept finding him, but he knew what would happen if he fell into a rift. He would end up somewhere else, in another dimension, and the other boy might not bring him back.

Jayden was on a mission. He had to get back home, back to his parents. Back to the district. Unlike the other kids at the compound, he had the means to do so. He just hadn't planned on going back so soon. He thought the other boy was his friend. That's why he told him what he planned to do. It was wrong to kill people, even ords. *Ugh!* Jayden hated that word. It wasn't their fault they didn't have powers. Jayden's parents were ords. He missed them every day. He regretted running off when they told him he couldn't visit his grandparents in Florida. He regretted trying to call his grandma anyway and getting lost in the phone line. Jayden was ten. His power wasn't fully developed, and he couldn't control it.

Six months later, he lived in a compound on the other side of the country, with other kids like him and a shadowy leader called the Liberator, who called everyone "Brother." It was fun, at first. Jayden learned a lot about using his power. But he also learned the Liberator was what ords called a *terrorist*. He killed people. He trained kids to kill people. That's when Jayden told the other boy his plan.

A rift opened in front of him, too large to avoid. In his electronic form, Jayden couldn't see the rift but he could sense the disruption in the impulses and cables. It was like waking up in his room back in the district and finding a hole in the wall, a hole that tried to suck him in. The only way he could avoid the rift was to create a hole of his own, to leave the netherfield. But was he close enough to the district?

Only one way to find out. He shifted his electronic form downwards. The hole opened, revealing a night sky. Jayden dove into it.

His electronic form solidified into a body and rolled around on the ground. Becoming human again always made Jayden dizzy, like being on a merry-go-round. When the images stopped spinning, he realized he had landed in the middle of the street. He recognized some of the older houses around him. He'd made it. He was back in the district.

A rift opened next to him.

He found me. Jayden didn't wait to see what dimension lay on the other side of the rift—whether it was rocks or gas or molten lava. He took off running.

He knew the area well enough, thanks to walks with his dad, to know where to go. Around the corner lay a stately government building with a flagpole in front. He ran up to the front door of district Surveillance Headquarters, Third Sector, and rapped on the door. But the building was closed for the night.

That was no problem for Jayden though. He'd learned a lot at the compound, including how to use his powers to disable security devices. All he had to do was enter the device and manipulate a few electrons. The door buzzed open.

Inside lay a row of cubicles with computers. Jayden hoped to run into a night watchman so he could turn himself in, but no such luck. He sat down at one of the computer terminals and easily manipulated it into turning itself on and overriding the password. He could send an email to the district police. No, that wouldn't work. He could use the soft phone to call home. He tried that, but the number was disconnected. *Oh, no. The Liberator must've been right. My parents must've had to move away from the district after I disappeared.* The district was for powered kids and their families. Without a powered kid, they couldn't stay. Jayden felt lost and confused. He wondered where his parents had moved. Back to Florida, he hoped.

A file on the desktop caught his eye. It read

"D. NEUMEYER/MACKINTOSH PARK INCIDENT/RAW FOOTAGE."

The name sounded familiar. The boy at the compound, Jayden's former friend, had mentioned a kid he called "Noo-meyer." The kid had gotten the rift-maker into trouble and made him escape from the district. He said that, if he ever got to go back to the district, he would make Noo-meyer pay. Curious, Jayden opened the file.

After watching the video in the file, Jayden smiled. He wondered if there were other videos of this Neumeyer. He found one and opened it.

"Don't cha know, breaking and entering's illegal," came a deep voice behind him.

Jayden spun around and looked into the coal-black eyes. Eyes he hoped he'd never see again.

"Calvin!"

"You know that stuff the Liberator's been feeding us? It's got enzymes that get into our bloodstream. He says they're like mini-computers. They allow him to track us. He don' like it when kids try to leave the compound."

The boy towered over Jayden, his grey shirt and pants almost identical to Jayden's, but Calvin had earned special privileges. He got to embroider his own name on his shirt and a design of his choosing. Calvin chose a skull. He sneered, the angular curve of his face reminding Jayden of a snake.

"There's something else about that food," Jayden spoke quickly, hoping to reason with Calvin.

"Shut up."

"There's a reason why I stopped eating it and sneaking food into the compound—"

"Shut up! The Liberator says t' teach you a lesson. He didn' say how long I had t' teach ya, though." He raised his hand.

"NO!" Jayden spun back to face the computer. Maybe he could get into it, get away. But there wasn't time. Hot air blasted him from below as the chair give way and fell into another dimension, taking Jayden with it.

~ * ~

Calvin waved his hand again, sealing the rift. He hated to do that to Jayden, but the kid broke the law. The Liberator's law. The only law that mattered.

Alone now, he looked across the dark office room, lit only by windows and the occasional light from a computer. It was a sterile, ordered environment, an *ord* environment. Calvin hated being back in the district. He started to open another rift to leave the way he came. But the computer Jayden had been sitting at glowed brighter than the rest. It played a video. Calvin hadn't seen a video in months—the Liberator didn't allow them. He wondered what Jayden was watching.

He peered closer to the screen and scowled as he saw a familiar face. "So, tha's how Noo-meyer did it. He wasn' alone." A plan hatched in Calvin's mind to make Damon—and anyone who helped him—pay.

Part I

Chapter One
The Dream

From the wide French windows, Damon could see rolling snow banks and snowflakes the size of golf balls. Inside the old-time Swiss chalet, he was warm. He sat at a large banquet table covered with a white table cloth and took a bite of orange-flavored waffles. Behind him, a fireplace crackled, bathing him in its warmth and light.

"Hey Damon!" said Vee Evans, who sat next to him, gobbling down a stack of twenty pancakes at super-speed. Vee looked like he was about six years old. He spoke while he ate, but Damon couldn't understand him. Across from him sat Danner Young, who had grown to a size of about seven feet tall, almost too big for the table. He laughed like a jolly Santa Claus. At the end of the table sat Ali Reeves and Denise Evans, Vee's sister. They laughed and exchanged gifts while Ali floated above the table and Denise's eyes were closed, as if she were dreaming of the future.

"Quite a place you have here," came a familiar voice. Across the table from Damon sat Kyle Powell. He looked older. His hair was longer, and the beginnings of a beard sprouted from his chin.

"Kyle," Damon shouted with delight, "how did you get here?"

"I drove."

"In your brother's Mustang?"

Kyle shrugged as if it was the obvious answer, and Damon felt bad for asking.

"Hey, everybody!" he shouted, "look who's here!"

But the others at the table continued to eat and talk as if Damon had said nothing.

"I don't belong here," Kyle said, looking sad.

Before Damon could ask what he meant, Vee interrupted. "Hey, Damon! Watch me steal something off of everyone's plate without them noticing." Vee turned into a blur and vanished from his chair. The super-fast kid moved around the table in slow-mo, and Damon wanted him to finish the practical joke so he could talk to Kyle.

But when Damon looked back for Kyle, instead he saw a small table sitting at the far end of the restaurant. Damon's parents and brother, Eldon, sat at a table, looking at large, book-like menus.

Damon wondered if he should go over and join them, but his dad looked up and grinned. It was the type of grin his dad used to make when Damon was very small—a grin that said, "You're doing fine, just keep it up." Damon hadn't seen that grin in a long time. He smiled back. He was exactly where he was supposed to be.

~ * ~

A buzz jolted him. He opened his eyes long enough to get his bearings and shut off the alarm clock.

"Damon!" his mother called from downstairs. "Time to get up. You don't want to be late for the bus."

Bus? In his groggy state, Damon struggled to remember what she meant. Only ords rode the bus. Ords like Eldon.

He opened his eyes and saw nothing. It was pitch black. A moment later, his night vision kicked in, and the alarm clock and table appeared in view, as well as the poster of a Swiss chalet on his wall, all reduced to black-and-white simplicity. Damon realized that his dark space had somehow activated itself while he was asleep. It had been doing that sometimes, ever since he had recovered from the null bomb's effects last year. He had gotten off lucky, unlike Kyle.

So far no one knew Damon's power had been acting up, and he wanted to keep it that way. The battery of tests he had undergone to restore his power to full strength was bad enough, but he couldn't live it down if word got out that he was losing his power. It would be okay on its own, in time.

He inhaled, and the dark space vanished on command. A brilliant morning light streamed into the room through the blinds near Damon's bed. He rolled over to go back to sleep.

The bus.

He bolted out of bed and fumbled for the red-and-white pullover and brand new jeans he'd laid out the night before. Eldon had teased him over being "fussy like a girl" for his first day at the new school, but Damon didn't care. His brother was still asleep, stirring in his own bed. If Damon were lucky, he'd get to sneak out without having to endure more teasing.

Damon didn't want Eldon to see how nervous he was. He had never ridden the bus before in his life. The old district school was just two blocks away. What idiot had decided to move the eighth grade to the high school? More kids with powers were being discovered, they were told, so the district had to expand. But Damon knew the real reason: It was just another excuse to hustle powered kids around with rules that didn't make any sense.

He ran downstairs and into the kitchen, where his mother had already prepared breakfast.

"Oh, cheer up!" she said, seeing his dour expression. "You're going to a new school. It will be a new adventure."

Damon gulped down the bacon and peppered scrambled eggs. He remembered Vee, gobbling down pancakes in the dream at the Swiss chalet, a place that existed only in Damon's imagination and somewhere on the other side of the world. Why couldn't the dream be real?

"Don't forget the toast," his mother said.

Damon hated toast, but he bit into it anyway to please her.

"Besides," she added, returning the conversation to the new school, "you'll be reunited with some of your old Power Club friends."

It was true. Danner, Ali, and Denise were starting their freshman year in high school. Only Vee, a seventh grader, still went to the old school.

"I won't have any classes with them," Damon mumbled.

"But you may see them in the hall or have lunch with them."

Damon pretended to smile.

"When's Dad coming home?"

"Now, Damon, you know your father works very hard for the district. He'll be home when he's home." She turned away, and Damon knew she was lying.

He finished breakfast, jumped up and grabbed his book bag, and headed for the door. His mother caught up him and gave him a hug and a kiss on the cheek.

"For good luck," she said.

Damon bolted out the door. He didn't want her to sense the truth. He dreaded seeing the others again. They had not parted on the best of terms. The Power Club now existed only in his dreams.

Chapter Two
The New School

A battered old school bus approached. Damon resented it and what it cost him.

Ever since first grade, Damon had wanted to be a crossing guard. He had dreamed of the day when he would enter the eighth grade wearing a helmet and badge and could stand on a street corner, telling other kids when to cross the street. Every kid at the old school wanted to be a crossing guard.

Riding the bus meant there would be no helmet or badge for him. The new school was too far away to employ kids as crossing guards.

As he climbed the stairs of the bus, the old driver, a man with glasses and a thick, grey beard, glared at him. "No powers on the bus!"

"I wasn't going to use my power," Damon shot back.

The driver shrugged. "I say that to every kid as they board. Saves trouble."

Damon turned to face the rows of seats, already half filled with kids. Most were from his old school, but there were a few he didn't know. Halfway down the aisle, Damon saw one friendly face: his old buddy, Andy. He had grown his hair out over the summer but was still the same round-faced boy with a perpetual football jersey. Today he also wore a heavy jacket even though it was the middle of August. Andy looked up and grinned, and Damon knew it was okay to sit with him.

"What's with the jacket?"

"It's because of my power," Andy replied, looking downcast. "The doctors say it's growing and I'll eventually get used to it, but right now I'm always cold."

"That's a good thing, right? That your power's growing?"

"I guess, but I'd still rather play football than have a stupid power."

Andy's abruptness made Damon wince. He had seen firsthand what any power could do and didn't think any of them were stupid. He changed the subject. "Say, where's Aric? You guys live so close I thought he'd get on the bus the same time as you."

Andy's eyebrows shot up. "Didn't you hear? The district sent him to some kind of early college for powered kids. They think his radar vision will be useful for the military. He and his whole family moved away about a month ago."

Damon stared in disbelief. Another friend had moved away, and he had missed it. He also felt strangely jealous. *If there's an early college for powered kids, I should be the one who goes there. I led the Power Club last year when we stopped a riot and a robbery!*

The district didn't want powered kids acting like heroes, Damon had been told. Apparently, being recruited for the military was different.

The bus drove through parts of the district Damon had seen before mainly on car rides with his parents. The bus went up the boulevard, through several neighborhoods and even past the old art gallery, a pillared, stately structure which had been there longer than the district.

"There it is!" Andy exclaimed, looking out the window. "There's the new school."

At the bottom of the valley stood a three-story brick building which resembled two buildings joined together in the center by a grey, H-shaped column that stretched up into a tower. The building overlooked a well-kept lawn and circular drive. The new school was much larger than the old one and, for a moment, Damon felt anxious about getting lost in it. His fears seemed to find form as the window of the bus became hazy and then crystallized into a sheet of ice.

"What happened?" Damon asked.

Andy looked embarrassed again. "Sorry," he said, as a frosty breath escaped from his nostrils and mouth. "It happens when I get nervous."

Frantically, Damon said, "Well, do something!" He remembered the driver's stern warning not to use powers on the bus.

Andy rubbed the ice with the elbow of his jacket. Damon strained to see through other windows and felt the dip as the bus entered a driveway and descended into the valley.

"They're taking us to the Freshmen Annex," someone said behind him.

"But we're not freshmen," someone else pointed out.

Andy finished rubbing the ice off the window just as the bus came to a halt. All Damon could see now was that they were in a parking lot behind the school. Damon looked around, trying to memorize some sort of escape route, though he wasn't sure why. Not being able to examine the school in every detail as they approached made him feel even more powerless and out of control. The bus doors whooshed open and everyone poured out.

~ * ~

The Freshman Annex turned out to be a smaller, more modern looking structure attached to the rear of the main building. Its flat roof and tinted glass façade revealed a sparse lobby and stairwell. It reminded Damon of the command center on his favorite TV show, *Star Seekers*, which had recently been cancelled, and it gave him some comfort to pretend he was a member of the crew on the show. "Lt. Neumeyer reporting for duty!" he imagined himself saying to the portly teacher who greeted them in the lobby. The teacher called the roll to make sure everyone was present and passed out locker combinations, class schedules, maps, and a list of school rules. "There are only ten minutes between classes," he announced in a nasal voice, "and right now, you have six and a half minutes to get to your first class."

As their classmates dispersed, Damon and Andy studied their schedules. Damon's heart sank. "We don't have any classes together."

"Maybe we can meet up for lunch," Andy offered.

Damon frowned. "I have third lunch period. You have first."

"Well, maybe we can hang out between classes sometime," Andy said. He turned to one of the wide hallways, and then he was gone.

Damon studied the map. As he started down another hallway, other kids swarmed about, chattering and yelling. The sounds of locker doors banging made him jump. Damon no longer felt like a lieutenant on a science fiction show. He was in the eighth grade now, but instead of being in the highest grade at the old school, he was in the lowest grade at the new school.

He was starting over.

Chapter Three
New Faces, Old Faces

"Watch it!"

Damon heard the warning a split second before he rounded a corner and collided with a wall. But this wall looked like a torso. He bounced back as if he'd landed face first on a trampoline and fell back on his butt. His books, class schedule, and map scattered across the floor.

A chorus of kids burst into laughter. *Terrific. First day of school and already I lool like a doof.* He looked up to see what he had hit.

The wall was in fact a torso. A towheaded youth towered over him like a mountain. Damon had never seen so many muscles, which rippled through the boy's arms as if he were a cartoon character. A long, thin face perched atop a massive torso. The boy wore a plain t-shirt with the sleeves rolled up so there was no mistaking that the muscles were his.

"That's what you get for not paying attention!" the youth said.

"I would," Damon fired back, "but I didn't expect to run into Mount Kilimanjaro!" He remembered Mount Kilimanjaro from geography class at the old school. Using humor might help him recover face.

The youth's smug expression turned into a hateful scowl. "I don't like smart-asses!" he said, as he stomped toward Damon. The floor shook. The boy grabbed Damon and lifted him up over his head. Damon felt a rush of blood as he stared down at other kids, who paused in the hallway to laugh at him.

He breathed in sharply. He could exhale—but what good would the dark space do him in this situation?

"Gareth Sanderson!" A shrill woman's voice cut through the air. Everyone in the hallway stopped moving. "Put him down. Gently."

The muscular boy obeyed like a wounded puppy. Damon looked

past him toward an open classroom door at the end of the hallway. In the doorway stood a young woman who looked as if she couldn't have been much older than a high school student. A basket weave of crimson hair drew back from a frail face and frail body. She wore a pale blue sweater and tan slacks which seemed too large for her. Yet there was no mistaking her commanding tone and gaze. She looked like a hawk ready to pounce on the towheaded boy. "There are rules governing the use of powers in this school. If you break one again, you will face another suspension."

The boy, Gareth, hung his head and muttered, "Yes, Miss Vogel." He closed his eyes, and, for a moment, Damon thought he might cry. However, the boy's massive torso and muscles softened and shrunk to the size of a normal boy about Damon's age. He slinked down the hallway and vanished into a sea of kids.

Damon scooped up his map, schedule, and bookbag. The teacher continued to stand in the doorway, eyeing Damon curiously. He felt he should say something.

"Are you Miss Vogel?"

She nodded. She was small for a teacher. Damon just about met her eyes. "If you've come for Language Arts, you're in the right place." She made a swooping gesture inside the classroom.

Damon fumbled for his schedule. "I think I have math first. I just wanted to say thanks...thank you," he corrected himself.

Her face broadened into a warm grin. "What do you know? A polite powered child. Well, you have about thirty seconds to get to class before the bell rings."

~ * ~

Damon made it to the math room a split second before the bell rang and grabbed a desk at the back of the class. If the teacher noticed him, he didn't say anything. Neither did the fifteen other students in the class. They all seemed enraptured as the teacher—a middle-aged man with slicked-back hair, a white shirt, and tie—related some anecdote about the importance of polynomials.

He looked around the room to see if there were any other familiar faces. A few kids from the old school were there, including a girl with rust-colored hair and turquoise glasses. Samantha Andrus. *Oh, great! The first class of the day with Sami the Snitch.* It wasn't her fault, she would remind everyone within earshot that her enhanced hearing could pick up everything that happened in an indeterminate radius, or that she needed to tell what she'd learned as soon as she learned it or she would go mad with overstimulation of noises. But Damon could never forgive her for overhearing his confession to a friend that he had a crush on Kendra Hawks in the fifth grade. Everybody teased Damon by saying "You devil, you!" Whenever Sami was around, you had to watch what you said.

In the front row sat a kid with shaggy blonde hair who looked familiar, but Damon couldn't place him.

The teacher wrote his name, "MR. KYTEL," on the whiteboard and began scribbling algebraic equations. "Oh, by the way," he said, turning to the class with a raised eyebrow, "now would be a good time to take notes."

Notebooks banged open, zippers unzipped, and pens were produced. Damon had to dig through his bookbag to find his pencil box, which had been shuffled around during his collision with Gareth. As he groped through the bag, he noticed the kid with the shaggy hair turn around and asked someone behind him if he could borrow a pencil. He was older now, but the snout-like nose and prominent molars were a dead giveaway.

Eddie Costa.

The boy from the Forbidden Neighborhood.

Even in the district, some powers were too dangerous. Kids with those powers lived in a section known as the Forbidden Neighborhood—forbidden because other kids weren't supposed to go there for any reason. Yet Damon had gotten lost one Halloween night and wandered into the Forbidden Neighborhood. He was attacked by skeletons and jack-o-lanterns—older kids whose powers consisted of the ability to change their appearance. Damon's dark space protected him, but he couldn't find his way out of the Forbidden Neighborhood. Then a werewolf showed up. And there he was. In the first row of math class.

~ * ~

Damon waited in the hall for Eddie to emerge from the classroom. As soon as he did, Damon called his name.

A glimmer of recognition crossed Eddie's face. "Hey, you're the kid with the darkness power! I'm glad you made it back to your own neighborhood."

"Well, thank you again for helping me, for scaring off the other kids."

Eddie seemed embarrassed. "Don't mention it."

"So, what are you doing here? I thought kids in the Forbidden Neighborhood couldn't attend regular school."

"We can once we learn how to control our powers," Eddie answered with pride. "Here, watch this!" He sat his books on the floor and shook his shoulders as if to limber up. Damon watched, amazed, as the shaggy hair grew even shaggier and turned dark, transforming into a fine fur. Eddie's small, flat nose rounded into a snout and fangs protruded from his mouth. The only trace of the boy which remained was his placid blue eyes.

The werewolf-headed boy roared at girls who passed by. Some screamed. Others laughed.

Damon watched all of this with knowing amusement. He'd seen this "trick" before—though, previously, Eddie's entire body had been covered in fur.

The werewolf reared back and shook its head. Almost instantly, it transformed back into Eddie.

"I used to break out of all my clothes," he boasted, "but now I can transform just a part of my body. The district says that's good enough for me to attend regular school."

"That's so cool!"

"What about you? What can you do with your dark space now?"

Damon thought about explaining how he could create a small dark space between his fingers—a universe of nothing, he'd called it—or that he could create multiple dark spaces at once. But that was all in the past.

"I'm not sure," he demurred. "I haven't really been practicing it."

He half expected Eddie to understand, like Andy, that powers were a burden. But Eddie looked confused. "Why not? If I had your power, I'd want to know what it can do. Darkness is awesome."

16

Damon felt himself blush. Eddie's genuineness made him feel good about his own power, even though it sometimes seemed useless.

"Hey, Damon!" a girl's voice called from behind him.

Grateful for the interruption, Damon turned to see who had called his name. He didn't recognize the voice at first and was surprised to see who it belonged to. Floating down the hallway toward him was Ali Reeves. She had shortened her dark brown hair since last year and seemed to be a couple of inches taller—but Damon realized she was literally walking on air. *Show off!* She wore a black leather jacket with red stripes stretching the length of each arm.

A torrent of emotions flooded him. Though he and Ali were never close, it had stung when she had quit the Power Club. Her email still echoed in his mind: *i'm quitting PC. i don't want to be a hero. i hope you understand.* He didn't understand, at least not then.

"Hey," she repeated as she "stepped off" the invisible cloud on which she had been walking and landed on the floor next to Damon.

"Hey." Damon echoed her casual tone.

"I know high schoolers aren't supposed to hang out with lowly eighth graders, but I had to stop and see what you're up to."

Damon shrugged, not sure what to say.

Eddie raised an eyebrow. "Hey, Damon, who's your friend?"

Damon made quick introductions.

Eddie looked Ali up and down. His interest seemed more than casual. "I may be an eighth grader," he said, "but that's only because living in the Forbidden Neighborhood put me back a year. I bet I'm the same age as you."

They compared birthdays and found they were only a week apart. Ali giggled.

Damon shifted his weight from one leg to the other, feeling as if he wasn't really part of this conversation.

"So, I wanted to ask you," Ali said, turning to him, "are you going to try out for the Safety Patrol?"

"The Safety Patrol?" Damon knew full well that the new school didn't recruit students to be crossing guards. Was she rubbing it in?

Picking up on his confusion, Ali said, "Where have you been all summer? Haven't you heard of us?" She gestured with both forefingers to a logo emblazoned on the chest of her black jacket. The logo consisted of a double gold triangle and the words SAFETY PATROL. Embroidered above it in a red cursive script: ALEJANDRA REEVES, OFFICIAL MEMBER.

Damon shook his head. "Is that supposed to mean something?"

Ali rolled her eyes. "I don't have time to explain. Just be in the courtyard in 15 minutes, 'kay? Bye!" She floated away as quickly as she had arrived.

He turned to Eddie. The other boy stared down the hallway, his mouth half open.

"There goes the girl of my dreams," Eddie said.

Chapter Four
The Safety Patrol

A screeching bell tone filled the hall. Damon jumped.

"That's just the intercom," Eddie said. "You'll get used to it."

"ATTENTION, ALL STUDENTS," a monotone voice boomed. "SECOND PERIOD CLASSES WILL BE DELAYED TWENTY MINUTES. PLEASE ASSEMBLE IN THE COURTYARD FOR A SPECIAL PRESENTATION."

The bell tone sounded again to announce the end of the message.

Eddie started to take off down the hallway. "I'm gonna put my books in my locker before the presentation."

"What presentation?" Damon was finding he didn't like surprises, and he'd had too many already this morning.

A strange smile crossed Eddie's face. It was the same kind of ogling smile he'd worn when he was looking at Ali.

"You'll see."

Damon fell in with other students who were lining up to descend the staircase and exit into the courtyard. He didn't want to look as ignorant as he felt about this special presentation, so he kept his books with him rather than tracking down his locker and being late to whatever awaited him outside. But as the line of students trickled down the staircase, Damon realized he hadn't been to the restroom since before he'd left home that morning. Maybe it was just nervousness and not knowing what to expect in the courtyard, but he was glad to see a boy's room at the bottom of the staircase.

He laid his books on the shelf of the long rectangular restroom when he heard a loud THUMP from one of the stalls.

"I told you to watch yourself!" came a familiar voice from inside the stall.

The kid in the hall! Gareth.

THUD! Damon saw the stall on the far end of the wall shake. Another boy cried, "Owww!"

Damon's heart raced as he headed for the restroom door. Reporting the incident to a teacher was the proper thing to do, what he had been told to do at the old school. But the new school was enormous, and he didn't know how far he'd have to go to find a teacher. *Besides, I know how to handle bullies.* He flashed back to the robbers at Anilora's grocery store and the riot at the mall last year. Compared to those situations, a muscle-bound bully was nothing.

He marched over to the stall and kicked in the door.

The door bounced against something massive and swung outward, revealing Gareth with his back to Damon. Muscles rippled from Gareth's arms and legs, and his massive fist had burrowed into the chest of another boy who appeared to be made of rubber. The boy's limbs flailed about like spaghetti, and his neck and chin stretched in ways Damon thought impossible.

Gareth looked over his shoulder, and Damon caught a momentary glimpse of fear at being caught.

"What the hell do you want?" he bellowed.

Damon arched his back like he'd seen heroes in movies do. In his most commanding voice he said, "Let him go!"

Gareth swung a leg around and planted it firmly on Damon's torso, just below his navel, and pushed outward. The kick sent Damon flying backwards but Damon was prepared for this.

He'd worked out similar moves with the Power Club last year. He pivoted around in mid-air and caught himself on the edge of the sink before he collided with it.

In the mirror above the sink, he saw Gareth barreling toward him. He expelled a breath from his mouth, and the restroom plunged into darkness. Damon leaped to his right as Gareth's hulking frame brushed past him and collided with the sink. There was a loud CRACK!

Creating the dark space so fast made Damon dizzy. He wandered around blind until his night vision activated. The restroom appeared before him in black and white, like an old-time movie. He saw Gareth slumped to the floor, holding his head with both hands, and whimpering. A spider-web of cracks decorated the mirror where Gareth hit it.

Oh, no! I hope I haven't hurt him. Damon inhaled, making the dark space vanish. As his vision returned to normal, he took a cautious step forward. Something flew out of the stall and slapped Damon in the forehead with such force that it knocked him off his feet. He caught a glimpse of something resembling a manta ray. The blob flattened itself, squeezed through the crack between the door and floor, and disappeared.

Damon ran to the stall. The rubbery boy was gone. *A shape shifter!*

Gareth jumped up from the floor. Other than a bruise on his forehead and a swollen nose, he seemed all right. "Who turned out the lights?"

"That's my power," Damon boasted. He prepared to exhale again. "I create darkness." He stood ready for anything.

Gareth glared at Damon. He glanced into the stall and then around the restroom. "You let him get away?"

"Well...yeah!"

"You stupid! Do you even know who that is or what he's doing here?"

Damon shook his head.

Gareth doubled his fist, and Damon prepared for the worst—but the other boy only slammed the door of another stall. "Mind your own business!" He stomped past Damon, flung the door open, and left.

~ * ~

There was nothing for Damon to do but join the presentation in the courtyard—or quad, as some kids called it. Still sore from where Gareth kicked him, he limped through the double glass doors and found an outdoors area surrounded on three sides by other parts of the school and on the fourth by what looked like a park barricaded by lush trees. A couple of hundred kids faced the park, and Damon saw movement over their heads. A loud roar reverberated from loudspeakers. *Oh, great. We're going to watch a horror movie.* The kids hollered and cheered.

Midway through the crowd, Damon spotted Eddie and made his way to him.

"So, what's so important?" Damon asked.

Eddie didn't take his eyes off whatever was in front of him. "Just watch."

Damon turned to face the park and saw something he hadn't seen in months. Danner Young, former member of the Power Club, the guy who could grow to huge heights, swayed back and forth between the trees at his maximum height of 30 feet—maybe a little taller. He was locked in what appeared to be a deadly struggle with a dragon.

"I know that guy!" Damon blurted before the full image of what he was seeing registered. Danner Young. The guy who quit the Power Club. The guy who nevertheless helped Kyle and Damon stop the robbery. The guy who always acted like a jerk. Fighting a dragon.

Damon shook his head. "Dragons don't exist."

The dragon's brown and orange scales glistened in the morning sun. A giant maw with jagged teeth snapped at Danner as the giant kid tried to keep a distance. But something seemed off. The dragon's movements were rigid, mechanical. Its large eyes, in the style of manga books, never blinked or changed expression. And something was off with Danner, as well. He seemed to be holding back.

"Hey, ugly!" a girl's voice shouted. "Follow me!"

Ali dove from one of the trees, flew between Danner and the dragon, made an arc, and flew away. The dragon—mechanical and slow—followed her.

"Man," Eddie said, his voice drifting along as if he were in a dream, "she's so graceful."

"Yeah," Damon echoed. A year ago, Ali was so awkward at using her power that she was afraid a great wind would blow her out of the district. Now she flew circles around the dragon like a pro.

Inexplicably, Ali slowed her flight and hovered in midair. The dragon stretched its maw, which was almost twice her size and lunged for the kill. Damon couldn't believe it. He was about to watch one of his teammates get eaten by a dragon and there was nothing he could do.

"NOW, RUS!" Danner shouted to someone on the ground.

A beam of golden light shot up from somewhere below. Damon couldn't see where the light came from, but it was all too familiar. His heart sank.

The light struck the dragon in the chest and expanded into a ring of fire that burned up the beast's torso, across its winged shoulders, and up to its maw, exposing circuitry and gears. The dragon let out a deafening howl and exploded.

Bits of dragon flew in every direction, including toward the crowd. Some kids screamed and started to run, but the dragon bits stopped in midair and bounced off a curtain—no, not a curtain. A translucent wall appeared out of nowhere. It seemed to be made of interlocking bricks. As soon as the dragon bits fell to the ground, the force field vanished.

The crowd burst into applause.

Damon struggled to process what he had just witnessed. Danner and Ali had just put on a show for the school. But why?

"Thank you very much," a man's voice boomed over the loudspeakers. Damon followed the gaze of the crowd as everyone turned to the left. There, at the edge of the park, he saw a raised podium. On the podium stood a man with grey-brown hair and wearing tinted glasses and a dark jacket similar to the one Ali had worn in the hallway. He spoke into a microphone. "Give it up one more time for the members of the Safety Patrol!"

The crowd erupted into applause and cheers again. Eddie raised his hands over his head and roared with approval. Damon felt disoriented and confused. He wanted to know what was going on.

The man made a gesture toward the park for someone to come and join him. Ali and Danner—who had shrunk back to his normal six-foot size—ran up to the podium. They were joined by a third kid—a boy whose scraggly blond hair was as unmistakable as his solar burst which had destroyed the dragon. Rusty Reddick.

In a way, it made sense. Rusty was the same age as Ali and Danner, so it seemed natural that he would join some new club that they would be part of. Then he and Danner could be jerks together. Damon hadn't forgotten that last year Rusty and two other boys, Calvin Goodrich and Larry Endicott, had jumped Damon in the alley behind his house. They used their powers to torture Damon for invading "their" territory. Damon fought back. He used his dark space to outwit them and drive them away. That's what earned him membership in the Power Club. But in his eyes, Rusty was still a "villain," and Ali and Danner were still "heroes." Watching them share a stage together bothered Damon.

The crowd quieted down as the man with the microphone resumed talking. "If you've seen the fliers around school and even around town for the last couple of months, you know the district has decided to do away with the old special clubs you could form in your neighborhoods."

Collective sounds of disapproval erupted from the crowd. Damon couldn't believe he'd heard correctly. His own special club—the Power Club—hadn't been active in months, but he now felt an incredible sense of loss. Special clubs were the way kids with powers got to work together, to use their powers freely, and to develop what they could do. It had taken Damon so long to join one, and now...

"But don't worry," the man said, raising his hand to silence the crowd. "The district has authorized a new kind of club, a school-sponsored club: the Safety Patrol." He gestured to Ali, Danner, and Rusty. "The club is still in its early stages, but, if you join, you will be part of a state-sponsored training program to help you hone and develop your powers. You will get to travel around and be a representative for powered kids everywhere—"

"Even outside the district?" someone in the crowd shouted.

"Yes, even outside the district," the man beamed.

Oohs and *aahs* went through the crowd. All powered kids wanted to leave the district, at least on short trips. Damon was no exception.

"And perhaps the best part," the man continued, "you get your very own official Safety Patrol jacket." He gestured to Ali, who had put her leather jacket with the red stripes back on and was displaying it for the crowd, sashaying back and forth like a runway model. Danner and Rusty picked up their jackets from behind the podium and put them on.

"How do we join?" someone else shouted.

The man's expression turned serious. "I won't lie to you. There is an application process, and not everyone will be accepted. We're looking for honor, integrity, good grades, and, of course, a power that you have already developed to some degree. If your power does not meet our standards, you can work with the teachers here at the school to get better control of it. Now," he glanced at his watch, "we've used up most of the twenty minutes allotted for this demonstration. Applications will be taken every day during school hours at my office—Dr. Adrian Stone, district liaison. The Safety Patrol will hang around for a few minutes to answer any questions." He nodded and left the stage.

Another voice boomed over the loudspeakers, ordering students to get to their next classes.

As the crowd dispersed, Eddie nudged Damon. "Come on! Let's go pick up applications."

Damon tried to take it all in. Danner and Ali had formed a new club. It was school-sponsored. It included Rusty. And it didn't include him. Damon didn't know why that bothered him. It's not like they were required to ask him. Yet the Power Club had been through a lot last year. It was more than just the club. It was where Damon had made friends. They had stopped a riot and a robbery. Without them, Damon felt like he was nothing.

Danner, Ali, and Rusty were each talking to several kids who had gathered around, but Danner excused himself and walked over to a retaining wall at the edge of the park to cool down. Damon saw his chance.

"You go on," he told Eddie. "I've got some questions of my own."

~ * ~

Damon felt like a stalker as he followed Danner to a grey stone wall at the edge of the quad, where Danner picked up a camouflage book bag.

"Hey, Danner," Damon started out, friendly.

"Damon." A curt reply. Danner started to walk away, but Damon wasn't going to let him off that easy.

"So, what's up with this Safety Patrol?"

Danner squinted. "Didn't you listen to the presentation?"

Damon didn't feel like explaining that he'd missed the first part of the presentation because he was busy preventing a kid from beating up on another kid—a thing heroes are supposed to do instead of putting on a show. Instead, he said, "I thought you and Ali were going to form a club just to have fun, because you didn't want to be heroes."

"We did," Danner replied. Then he tottered on his feet as if his book bag were suddenly too heavy. Damon guessed he was trying to decide if he wanted to give Damon more of an answer. Finally, almost in resignation, he dropped the book bag to the ground. "Look, the district came to me. They knew what we did at Anilora's."

"They did?" Stopping the robbery had been the Power Club's greatest achievement—and its greatest secret. The district didn't want powered kids to be heroes.

Danner waved his hand. "They didn't care so long as it didn't go public. But we showed them something. We showed them that powered kids could make a difference. So Doc Stone came to me and asked me to start a new club, one that would be sanctioned by the school and by the district. That way we could get kids to think about using their powers for good."

Damon reeled at the revelation. The Power Club taught the district something. They had made a difference. A feeling of pride welled up inside him. "But why did they come to you? I was the leader. You weren't even a member of the Power Club when we..." He started to say "broke up" but couldn't form the words.

Danner shrugged. "When your dad's a district police officer, you have all kinds of connections. Look, I'd love to chat, but I've got things to do." He hoisted the bag again.

Damon had to lay it out there. It was now or never. "So, what about me? Why didn't you ask me to join the Safety Patrol?"

Danner scrunched up his face as if it was the dumbest question ever. "You're not entitled, dumbass. You have to try out, just like everybody else."

The "entitled" remark hurt. Damon started to press his case when Rusty interrupted.

"Hey, Danner!" the scraggly-haired boy called as he approached. "Doc Stone wants us to go over some of the applications after school."

Danner nodded.

Still pierced by the "entitled" comment, Damon resented Rusty's intrusion even more—this kid who had jumped him in the alley and now was a member of the Safety Patrol, the state-sponsored club, the only club. This kid who was treated as a hero, while Damon was...nothing.

Damon swallowed his emotions. He could be the bigger man if he had to be. "Hey, Rusty," he said, trying to sound as friendly as he could muster.

Rusty's face scrunched up as if he smelled something disgusting. He turned to Danner. "Are we gonna let *him* join?"

Danner looked superior as he glanced at Damon. "Depends."

Chapter Five
A Rejection and a Warning

Damon floated through the next two hours of classes. He couldn't wait to get to lunch—he wished he'd eaten more of the breakfast his mother had cooked for him that morning. But, more, he tried to process everything he had learned. The Power Club actually had made a difference. Not only had they stopped a robbery, but the district thought it was a good idea that kids could be heroes. That's why they started the Safety Patrol.

But the Safety Patrol didn't include Damon.

Did he really think he was "entitled" to join? No, of course not. But Danner knew what Damon could do. He knew how powerful the dark space could be. And so did Ali. Why did they let Rusty join and not him?

He struggled to stay focused on his classes but really just wanted to make it to lunch. The cafeteria was not like he expected it to be. The gym at the old school doubled as cafeteria, so Damon was used to eating on fold-out tables that sat below basketball nets. But this cafeteria was large and spacious. Paintings of flowers and doorways and castles adorned the walls. Each painting had a plaque with the name of an artist underneath. Damon felt like he was in an art gallery.

Damon slipped into the serving line, bought a slice of pizza, an apple, and a soft drink with the money he had left over from his summer allowance. He thought maybe he could sit with kids from the old school, but he spied a vacant round, wooden table. It was too good to pass up, so he took it.

"They turned me down!" The chair next to Damon skidded as someone yanked it. A book bag landed in the center of the table, nearly crushing his slice of pizza. Damon looked up just in time to see Eddie plop down in the chair.

"Who?"

"The Safety Patrol. Dr. Stone saw my medical records. He said he wasn't sure I could control my 'feral tendencies' when I'm in full werewolf mode." Eddie hunched forward on the table. "Guess he's afraid I'll eat other kids."

"Would you?" Damon intended it as an innocent question, but, as the words escaped his mouth, he realized how little he knew about Eddie and about being a werewolf.

Eddie looked dead earnest. "Werewolves don't eat people. They only eat pets."

Damon stared.

"Fooled ya!" Eddie's mouth broadened into a wide grin, revealing his extra-large molars. Even in human form, he looked like an animal ready to pounce on its prey. "The district cleared me. They said I can control my power enough to go to school with regular kids. But, man, it sucks that I can't join the only special club."

Damon didn't know what impressed him more, that other powered kids could be considered "regular kids" or that Eddie wanted so badly to join a special club. He wondered what life must have been like in the Forbidden Neighborhood, where kids really couldn't do anything or go anywhere. Just because they were born with certain powers.

"What about you?" Eddie asked. "Did you try out?"

"No," Damon admitted.

"Why not?"

"Danner and I have history." It was true, but not the full truth. Damon still smarted from the "entitled" comment and didn't want to talk about it. "Besides, I was already part of a special club." He shrugged as if it were no big deal.

"You were?" Eddie's jaw dropped. "What was it like?"

~ * ~

After lunch, Damon decided to explore the school grounds. He asked Eddie to come with him, but Eddie said he had to go to the nurse's office. Damon wondered if this had something to do with Dr. Stone's concern about Eddie not being able to control his "feral tendencies" but did not ask.

Compared to the old school, the new school grounds were huge. They opened into a football field with goalposts under construction. The district had always spared no expense to give powered kids as normal a life as possible, but something about the football field didn't sit right with Damon. Just how many powered kids existed? How many did the district expect to go to school here? And how did the school plan to teach football to kids who could run at super-speed or fly or were super-strong?

Damon recalled how Andy had said that having a power was a burden and that he would rather play football like a normal kid. Was this what the district wanted? For kids to hate their powers so much they wanted to be ordinary? After his experiences last year, Damon wouldn't put anything past the district.

He returned to the school building through the quad just as he heard the bell ring, announcing he had ten minutes to get to his next class. Barring his path was a sickly-looking tree with yellowish bark and brown leaves. It was so unusual Damon wondered why he hadn't noticed it before. As he walked round the tree, one of its limbs swayed toward him. Damon hadn't noticed a breeze—especially one strong enough to move a tree limb. The limb expanded, taking on the shape of an arm with long, skeletal fingers which wrapped around Damon's torso and hoisted him in the air like an ant.

Damon opened his mouth to cry out, but a voice nearby said, "Shh!" The tree limbs rotated him to face the trunk. To his astonishment, the knots in the trunk moved like swirly lines until they formed a face—a face Damon recognized. It was the boy Gareth was beating up in the restroom. "Not one word," a deep voice spoke, "or I'll snap your neck like a twig!"

Damon struggled to look down. He was far enough off the ground that the fall might break his leg or worse.

"Now," the voice from the tree said, "what is your connection with Gareth Sanderson?"

"Wh-what?" Damon replied.

"Don't deny it!" The branches tightened around Damon's torso. "Why did you help him this morning?"

"I didn't! I was *trying* to help you!"

The tree face twisted into a grin. "Playing hero, huh? Well, don't. There are things going on at this school you don't know about, things that can get you killed."

The branches loosened their grip, and Damon started to fall. He grabbed on to one of the branches.

"You won't tell anyone about this," the face in the tree said. "No one will believe you." The branch lowered Damon a few feet and then dissolved into a foam-like substance.

Damon fell the rest of the way. He landed on his hands and knees— a jolt that left him more humiliated than hurt. He scrambled around to do...what, exactly, he wasn't sure. How would his dark space help him fight a tree?

The tree, however, was no longer there. It reshaped itself into a large, black bird which flapped its wings and darted toward him. He ducked.

"By the way," the bird said, "Calvin says hi."

Chapter Six
A Vision

Damon's heart pounded from racing up the stairs. It wasn't hard to find Dr. Stone's office. Posters littered almost every wall of the main school building and directed students to the third floor, urging them to apply for the Safety Patrol. Damon figured that's where he could find Danner and Ali. They knew about Calvin and could verify Damon's story.

As he reached the third floor, he stopped cold. The line of students waiting outside Dr. Stone's office stretched half the length of the hallway.

Panting, he asked the kid at the end of the line, "Why's everybody here?"

A freckly faced boy spun around. "To turn in our applications." He held up a single sheet of paper with printed text boxes and hand-scrawled answers.

So, this is what it's come to? Joining the only club is like applying for a job? A year ago, all Damon had to do was try to beat the members of the Power Club with his own power. Even though they rejected him at first, he loved the idea of just showing them what he could do.

Making kids fill out paperwork to join a club seemed weird. But none of that mattered now that Calvin was back. Damon took a deep breath and marched down the line.

"Hey!" someone yelled. "Go to the back of the line!"

Damon ignored taunts and jeers until a kid stepped out of the line in front of him and transformed into a large, flat, metallic substance barring his path. "Back of the line!" the kid bellowed through a mouth that had formed in the shiny, metallic surface.

"You don't understand," Damon protested.

"We've been waiting for an hour!" a girl shouted. "We had to get special permission to leave class. Where's your hall pass?" She held up her application and a yellow card attached to it.

"I don't have a hall pass. There's a kid who—"

"Then get to the BACK OF THE LIIIIIINNNNE!" The girl's voice reverberated like a thing of force, pushing Damon back against the wall. His ears throbbed. Another sonic attack, he feared, might puncture his eardrums.

Damon weighed his options. He could wait at the back of the line, like he was told, but what would he say when he got to the front? "Oh, by the way, there's a tree-boy who threatened me and he said Calvin's back— you know, Calvin, who can make people disappear and who could probably make the entire school disappear by now. Sorry I didn't tell you this earlier, but I had to wait at the back of the line."

No, that was not acceptable. Damon would have to do the right thing, even if it meant cutting in line. He examined the queue of kids who were jeering at him. His dark space could cover most of the line. In the confusion, he could slip past them and make his way to the office. He inhaled and prepared to release the deepest, darkest space any of these kids had ever seen.

"Damon!" a girl's voice called from near the stairwell. "I knew you'd be here."

He whirled around, and his heart leapt at the sight of a familiar face—someone he hadn't seen in almost a year. She was taller now, and her blonde hair was pulled back into a pony tail, but the same piercing blue eyes still commanded his attention. She wore a blue and white basketball jersey and shorts and was sweating as if she had run all the way from the gym, wherever it was located.

"Denise!" he said, unable to contain his relief at seeing her. "What are you doing here?"

She folded her arms as if Damon should know better than to ask. "Like I said, I knew you'd be here."

~ * ~

Denise led him to a secluded hallway. It contained no posters or windows, only large double doors with a sign that read THEATRE AUDITIONS—QUIET. *This school has a theatre, too?* Like the football field, Damon didn't see the point. The district was trying too hard to give powered kids a "normal" life, but how can you be normal when you can create darkness or see the future?

He turned to Denise to ask what was going on, but she raised her finger to indicate he should be quiet while she looked around to make sure they were alone. Finally, she turned to him.

"Don't try out for the Safety Patrol."

Damon's jaw dropped. He still didn't know if he wanted to apply. "Why not? Did you have a vision that they will reject me, just like you had a vision that I would be there?"

She shook her head. "They're not what you think they are. They're going to do presentations like the one in the quad and charity events, but Doc Stone won't let them be real heroes."

"But Danner said—"

"He doesn't know. Neither does Ali."

Damon stared at her, trying to let her words sink in. Why, he wondered, did she come all this way just to tell him that? "Is that why you didn't join?"

She looked away, as if ashamed. "I did try out. They turned me down. They said my power isn't accurate enough. But, Damon, that's not true. My visions always come true. You know it."

Damon sensed that she wanted him to nod or say yes or somehow validate the truth of her statement—and it was true. Denise could predict the future, but her visions weren't always precise. Even she had told him that. Last year, she had predicted the robbery at Anilora's and even knew when it was going to happen—but she didn't know how it would turn out. That's why she didn't show up—or her brother. The Power Club could have used Vee's super-speed to stop the robbers. If Vee had been there, he could have grabbed the null grenade and whisked it away before it went off. Kyle wouldn't have lost his power.

"Is that why you don't want me to try out? Because you couldn't make it?"

Denise looked stunned. "No, why would I care?"

"Then why—?"

"Because you're going to start another club."

Damon couldn't believe he heard her right. He had never started a club in his life. Besides, starting clubs was no longer allowed. "Yeah, right," he chortled and started to turn away.

"You're going to start a club," she insisted. "I've seen it."

Damon hated it when Denise said things like that. It was like having a bossy sister who was always right—except she *was* always right because she had seen the future.

"Okay, so I'm going to start a club," he said in a matter-of-fact tone, as if she'd just told him he was going to clean his room. "Who's going to be in it?"

"I don't know," she said.

"I don't want to start a club," he declared. "I'm through with clubs."

He thought she might insist again that her visions were never wrong, and he could point out they weren't always complete—maybe she had seen someone else start a club, someone who only looked like Damon. Instead she looked him straight in the eye with the most intense expression he had ever seen.

"Do you want to know why you're going to start a club?" she said.

Damon knew he probably shouldn't ask. He should probably just walk away and leave her alone with her visions. But the curiosity was too much for him. "Why?" he asked.

"Because you're the only one who can stop Calvin."

Damon felt light-headed. He needed to sit down, but there were no chairs or benches in this hallway. He settled for leaning against the wall next to the double doors with the theatre sign.

"What did you say?"

"You're the only one who can save us from Calvin." Her voice quivered, and he saw something in her eyes he had never seen before: terror.

"What do you mean 'us'?"

Denise started to speak, but the bell rang. Damon realized he was late to his next class. Denise shook her head and blinked, as if she had just come out of a trance. "Oh, no! I ran out of gym class when I had my vision of you. Now, I've got to go back to the gym on the first floor, shower, change, pick up my books in my locker, and go to my next class! I'll probably get detention on the first day of high school!" She turned and started to flitter down the hallway.

Damon couldn't move. His legs felt numb. "Denise, wait!"

She turned and pretended to push buttons on an imaginary phone. "Text me tonight." And she was gone before Damon could tell her he didn't have a phone.

Chapter Seven
Miss Vogel's Class

"I got lost," Damon said in the doorway.

Miss Vogel looked up from her desk, her eyebrows arching above her horn-rimmed glasses. "Two fights on the first day of school. This does not bode well for you."

"H-How did you know?" Damon stammered. He had told no one, not even Denise, about the tree-boy's threat.

Miss Vogel looked him over. "Children don't often show up in my class with their shirts hanging out and grass stains on their jeans."

The class burst into laughter.

Damon resisted the impulse to run away. Being laughed at was almost too much to bear after being threatened, being told he would start a new club, and twice hearing that Calvin was back. Damon's entire world seemed to dissolve into a state of uncertainty.

"That's enough!" Miss Vogel barked, her voice echoing off the walls like a siren. Everyone stopped laughing. "For future reference," she said to Damon, "you will need a hall pass if you are late to class. Since this is the first day, I will let it go. Please, take a seat."

Something in her voice reassured Damon, and he no longer felt like running. Not many teachers could get that many kids to stop laughing with two words. He made his way to a desk in the third row and sat down. Only then did he notice that sitting next to him was Sami the Snitch. Sami crinkled up her nose and glared at Damon in that way she had of indicating that she couldn't wait to tell the entire school about Damon's embarrassment. *Oh, great. Two classes with Sami. This is going to be a horrible year.*

Miss Vogel rose from her desk. "As I started to say," she told the class, "we will cover many subjects this semester, including mythology, current events, and literature. My goal is for each of you to see that people with special abilities have always been part of our culture. They have shaped our thinking and transformed our world."

Sami's hand shot up. When the teacher called on her, she said, "But, Miss Vogel, none of those people had powers."

"That is correct, Sami," the teacher replied, a sly grin crossing her lips. "At least most of them didn't."

"Most?" another kid asked.

"What if I told you," the teacher replied, "that not all powered people live in the district?"

A collective gasp crossed the room.

"What if I also told you that not all kids have to give up their powers when they leave the district?"

A boy raised his hand. "You're scamming us, aren't you, Miss Vogel?"

"Not at all," she replied, "but let me prove it to you. You know that all teachers who teach in the district must be certified at the state capital, don't you?"

The class nodded.

"And you know this certification takes up to two years after college, so you will grant me that I've lived outside the district for a considerable period of time, yes?"

More nods.

Damon wondered where she was going with this, and the notion made him uncomfortable.

"Well, in that case," the teacher said, "watch this." She carefully removed her jacket and laid it across her desk. Damon could see that her blouse contained no sleeves, only her bare arms—which were thin, fragile, almost emaciated. "My arms have to be this way," she said, anticipating their questions, "for me to do this." She stretched her arms out to her side and shook them once. A flapping sound reverberated across the classroom as her arms transformed into peacock-colored wings—a delicate pattern of greens and reds and oranges.

The class erupted into gasps of delight.

Damon stared in disbelief. Miss Vogel—a teacher—had a power. She had lived outside the district. Damon now understood why he felt uncomfortable. The only powered people he knew of who lived outside the district were terrorists.

~ * ~

Over supper, Damon gave terse answers to his mother's questions about his first day of school. He told her how big the school was, where his locker was located, and what the teachers were like. He said nothing about Gareth Sanderson, tree boy, or Miss Vogel having a power. He didn't want to answer a string of questions that would lead to him revealing what the tree boy or Denise had said. His mother would insist on calling the principal, but what would Damon tell the principal—that some unknown shape shifter had threatened him and that a girl who can see the future told him he would form a now illegal club?

For once, he was happy to let Eldon, who had started sixth grade at a school outside the district, regale his mother with every detail of his day.

After supper, Damon beat his brother to the den, where awaited the family computer—the only one his mother allowed them to have. Eldon could play Doom Squad later. Damon opened the secret folder he'd kept hidden since last year. He didn't know why he kept it, but he was glad he did. He opened the folder, revealing the email addresses of each former member of the Power Club and clicked on the chat feature next to one.

Denise are u there

He waited. After several seconds, he was about to give up when a "doink!" sound announced a new message.

Hi, Damon.

Hi. What did you mean about me saving u?

I can't go into it in detail. But Calvin's coming back. He's going to send us

somewhere. a desert, maybe,
IDK. There will be a lot of
sand.

Sand. Damon remembered the orange dimension in which Calvin had trapped him last year.

Besides u, who else is he coming after?

Danner and Ali. Maybe Vee, too. He knows we helped you at the park last year.

How does he know that?? Danner and Ali weren't even there

IDK

Maybe we should warn them.

They won't believe you.

But they will believe u. U and Ali are friends.

Were friends. She doesn't have time for me now that she's in the Safety Patrol.

I'm sorry.

Thx. Damon, forming another club is the only way.

Damon sat back in his chair. He felt cold all over. He had no idea who to even ask to join this club, and, how would he ask them? "Guess what? I want you to join a new club. It'll probably be illegal, and we'll be in danger. We'll be going up against a kid who can send us away forever, but, hey, you should join anyway."

Another thought occurred to him.

Do u know anything about Miss Vogel?

The Lang Arts teacher?
Sure. I have her for second
period. She's cool.

She has a power.

I know. It's awesome!!

How can she have a
power and live outside the
district?

She did some sort of special
service for the district.
Worked as a journalist, I
think. Why?

So, she's not a terrorist

No silly. 😊

At least that was something Damon didn't have to worry about. He wrote back that they should meet up at school to go over possible candidates for this new club. Denise probably knew more kids than he did. But before he could type, a message "doinked."

I can't help you find
members. ☹
One more thing. The new club
must be a secret.

Chapter Eight
Recruitment Drive

Damon stared at his poster of the Swiss chalet. He had never been to Switzerland and never thought he could go. The poster had been a rescue project, as his mother put it. The district library threw away a bunch of stuff, and Damon saw the image of a snowy embankment that looked like it was covered in an endless stream of pillows. In the middle of the embankment stood a chalet—a triangle-shaped roof covering a porch and house made of wood. Warm light emanated from the windows and Damon could just imagine a family having dinner, telling each other stories, and then going out to ride their sleds—things he could never do in the district. He told his mother that such of work of art should not be discarded and begged her to ask the librarian if he could take it.

In truth, the poster made him feel comfortable and warm and free every time he saw it, but he would never admit to such feelings. It had hung above his bed for five years now, and every time he felt lost or alone, he gazed at the chalet and daydreamed.

He chided himself. He should be thinking about who he could ask to join this new club—the secret club. Every kid he knew at school had a power; but most, like Andy's, weren't useful, good or easy to control. Just what kind of powers would he need to fight Calvin—and a shape changer? How do you fight a shape changer?

With another shape changer!

The idea was so simple, it was obvious. He rolled over and closed his eyes. He knew the first person he would ask. He just hoped he'd say yes.

~ * ~

The next day, Damon hurried off the bus, grabbed his books from his locker, and made his way to the math class before the first bell rang. To his relief, his target was sitting just where he had been yesterday—in the front row. *Dork! Don't you know cool kids sit in the rear?* Dork or not, Eddie Costa was his man.

Damon grabbed the seat behind Eddie.

"Hey, Eddie."

"Hey, D."

"D?"

"Short for Damon. I hope you don't mind." Eddie looked almost hurt, as if the slightest rejection might cause him to fall apart.

"N-No, not at all. Listen, there's somethi—"

"You can call me E."

"All right...E." The whole thing sounded childish to Damon, but if that's what it took to recruit Eddie, so be it. "Listen, there's something I need to ask you."

Eddie, who had been looking at Damon over his shoulder, spun around in his chair, as if he was unused to anyone asking him anything. Other kids started to spill into the room, so Damon would have to be quick.

"I know we're not allowed to have special clubs anymore," Damon spoke quietly, "but I wondered if you would be interested in starting one." He waited for some hint of interest from Eddie, but, when none emerged, he continued: "This isn't just any ordinary club, it's a club with a purpose. There's a guy named Calvin who caused a lot of trouble last year. He's back, and—"

There was a sudden scraping sound across the room, as if a chair were being forced backwards. Damon looked up just in time to see Samantha Andrus jump out of the chair and head his way. *Oh, great! Why did I have to open my mouth in front of Sami the Snitch?*

Sami beat out a boy who tried to take the seat next to Damon.

"I'm in!" she said in a low but determined voice.

Damon feigned ignorance. "In...what?"

Sami looked over the rim of her glasses, her eyes darting back and forth between Damon and Eddie. "I heard what you said about starting a new club. I also heard you mention Calvin. If you're going to do something about him, I want in." She spoke so fast and with such certainty that Damon imagined her words to be machine gun bullets. "Did you know that Suzy Steele was a friend of mine?"

"Who's Suzy Steele?" Eddie managed to squeeze in.

Sami told him about Suzy, who lived up to her name. She could transform her body into something resembling indestructible armor. But she and Calvin didn't get along. In the second grade, he opened a hole in the ground to make Suzy disappear. No one ever saw her again. "Calvin said he couldn't remember where he sent her. The creep! All I know is Suzy's gone, forever. So, if you guys are starting a club to do something about him, I want in."

The second bell rang. Sami jumped up and returned to her original seat before Mr. Kytel called the roll. Damon sat there in a daze. He wanted to recruit a werewolf. Instead, he got a girl with super-hearing and a grudge.

As the teacher called the class to order, Eddie leaned back. "Hey, D. Tell me more about this special club at lunch."

~ * ~

Damon returned to his locker, retrieved the lunch his mother had made him and hurried to the cafeteria. Since he brought his own lunch he didn't have to stand in line—though he'd have to get something to drink. He decided to grab the table first—the large, round one he'd eaten at yesterday—and wait for Eddie to show up.

But Eddie was already there—in the line for hot lunch. Damon tried to get his attention, but Eddie appeared to be haggling with a server over meatloaf. *Maybe he doesn't have enough money.* Damon reached into his bag and pulled out a peanut butter sandwich and an apple. *Seriously, Mom?* He stole furtive glances at other kids who were enjoying pastas, chili dogs, and even salads—and hoped no one would notice him eating a meal he brought from home, a meal he should have outgrown in the sixth grade.

The chair next to him screeched across the floor, and he looked up to see Sami carrying a hot lunch tray that included a veggie wrap, bowl of fruit, and a glass of ice water. She sat the tray on the table, almost tantalizingly in front of Damon, and scooted herself into the table. "What are you eating, Damon?"

"Just stuff," he said, hiding the peanut butter sandwich behind the paper bag as much as possible. The apple, he figured, was safe from scorn.

"So, who else is going to be in this new club of yours?"

"Shh!" he whispered. "It's supposed to be a secret."

Sami formed her mouth into a tight circle, indicating she understood and was glad to be part of his conspiracy. But Damon knew Sami too well. It was a huge gamble to take her into his confidence. He wouldn't mind if she got offended by his brusque demeanor and left. But she sat there and removed the cellophane from her veggie wrap.

Looking for something to say, Damon said, "I didn't know you and Suzy were friends." He was searching for something, trying to gauge her real interest in joining the club.

"She was my best friend," was all Sami offered. "But you didn't answer my question. Who else is joining the club?"

"Well..." Damon didn't know how to admit he didn't have anyone else yet. He had spent the morning observing other kids for signs of powers that might be useful. But the school had a strict rule against using powers in the hallways or classrooms. There were designated "power places"—like smoking areas—but Damon hadn't seen any kids he knew there. He really wanted to ask kids he already knew, but most had lame powers. At least Sami's super-hearing could prove useful. "That's something we need to talk about when Eddie gets here."

The clatter of a tray on the table announced Eddie's arrival. Instead of meatloaf, it consisted of a small bowl of potato salad and an oatmeal cookie. "I left my wallet at home," said Eddie. "This is all they would give me on credit. Some school!" He sat in the seat to Damon's right, looked over his shoulder at the servers, and said loudly, "If kids pass out from hunger, there will be lawsuits, you know!" He then turned to Damon and Sami and said, "How's it going, D and S?"

"S?" Sami said, frowning.

"It's short for Samantha."

"I know what it's short for. But we're not going to use code names, are we?"

Eddie looked hurt. "No, it's just a thing."

"A thing?"

"You know, a *thing* thing."

Damon and Sami glanced at each other. He was glad somebody else appeared clueless.

"Look, about this club," Damon spoke quietly, "you both have to know what we're up against."

Sami gave Damon her full attention, but Eddie dove into his potato salad and cookie, taking a bite of one and then the other. Damon told them about the Power Club's exploits of the previous year. Since the district knew they had stopped the robbery at Anilora's, he figured there was no reason to keep it a secret. He also told them about his run-in with Calvin.

"So, Calvin can make people disappear forever?" Eddie said between bites of food. There was a hint of fear in his voice.

"He sends them to other dimensions," Damon clarified. "And he can bring them back, if he wants to."

"Why doesn't the district send him to Alaska, where they keep the kids who misuse their powers?"

"I think the district tried," Damon admitted, "but he escaped."

"How do you know?" Sami asked. It was a legitimate question. How would Damon know what the district did after they arrested Calvin, or that he had escaped? *Because a man and a woman in the hospital told me so, but they also swore me to secrecy.* But the district had betrayed Damon by trying to discredit him, by spreading lies about what his dark space could do. Was he still under obligation to keep his promise? He wasn't sure.

But he could tell them what Denise had said, and about his encounter with the tree boy.

"Tree boy." Eddie pondered. "There used to be a guy in the Forbidden Neighborhood who could imitate trees and animals. I wonder if it's the same guy."

"So, Calvin is working with the tree boy, or the tree boy is working with Calvin?" Sami hunched forward, making herself small, and Damon thought she might disappear under the table. "What do you suppose he meant, that there are things going on at this school that can get you killed,

Damon?" It seemed like more than just a casual request for more information. Sami sounded genuinely concerned about Damon.

"I don't know. But the main thing is he's going after the former Power Club members for revenge. That's why we have to stop him. The main reason, anyway."

"But why?" Eddie asked. "I don't know these Power Club kids, but it sounds like they weren't nice to you. They broke up and left you. Why do you care what happens to them?"

The question threw Damon. He had never really considered it before. The obvious answer was that if Calvin was coming after them, he would come after Damon, too. But that wasn't it. At least not all of it. "Have you ever been a part of something that's larger than yourself?" he asked. "When we stopped the robbery, and even before that, when we fought the rioters at the mall, I felt like I was part of something that mattered. We all were. Friends or not, they're part of who I am now, and I'm part of them. I can't just let something bad happened to them. I can't! I've got to do this, whether you help me or not." The last bit was macho posturing and Damon getting carried away. But he meant what he said. Even he was surprised at what came out.

"You already know I'm in," Sami said in a solemn tone. "I didn't get to do those things with Suzy, but we were close. You should have seen her family when they realized she wasn't coming back. They were devastated."

"I'm in, too," Eddie said. "I never got to join a special club. I want to be part of something that matters."

Damon couldn't believe it. It was that easy! The club was happening, just like Denise said. Trying to keep his cool, he said, "Great! Any other questions?"

Eddie ogled the peanut butter sandwich. "Are you going to eat that?"

~ * ~

Great News!!! I've recruited two people.

Damon couldn't get on the computer until his brother took a break from Doom Squad. He wondered if he was too late, if Denise had gone to bed.

That's wonderful!

Damon smiled when her message popped up. He gave her a brief rundown of Eddie and Sami—their powers, what classes he had with them, how they came to join the club. Denise wrote back that she remembered Sami from the old school, but she didn't know Eddie. Damon felt he needed to play up Eddie's qualifications for joining the club.

Not only can he turn into a werewolf, he says he knows a guy who might be interested in joining the club. Sami says she knows someone, too.

You should keep the club small, Damon. Don't bring in too many people you don't know well. You never know who you can trust.

It was such an obvious point that Damon was horrified he hadn't thought of it. "Tree boy" could be anywhere or anyone, for all he knew. Damon suddenly felt insecure and not up to the task of starting a new club, particularly one that would be going up against Calvin and "Tree boy." He needed someone who could think ahead. He needed Denise.

Eddie said we can meet at his house. It's on the border of where the Forbidden Neighborhood used to be. Maybe you can

come and meet the others???

Great! I'd like that, Damon.

Chapter Nine
The Secret Club

Damon stared at the mansion before him. *Mansion?* It stood two stories tall and seemed impossibly wide—easily twice the width of Damon's own home. Four white pillars supported the overhang of the front porch, which held court above a circular drive. A cobblestone path snaked through an immaculate lawn. Damon's own lawn never looked so good, not even when his dad was home to take care of it.

Damon studied the address scrawled on a scrap of paper. The last digit could be either a 3 or an 8. That's it. Damon must have the wrong address. He looked around, wondering where 5203 could be.

"Psst!" someone called from nearby.

Banking the edge of the circular drive was a large, dark wood fence with planks that jutted into the sky like swords. Behind a partially open door, Sami beckoned him.

Eddie lives here? No way.

As he jogged to the door, he saw someone behind the fence whisper in Sami's ear. Sami shut the door.

"What's the password?" she said through a space in the planks.

Confused, Damon said, "We don't have a password."

"If we're going to have a secret club, we must have a password!"

Damon searched his memory. Did Sami or Eddie say anything about a password when they'd had lunch the day before or even today? Damon certainly hadn't. "Um, power," he guessed.

"Bzzt!" Sami pretended to make the sound of a buzzer. "You only get two more guesses!"

Was this a joke, or was it some ritual of Eddie's to gain admittance into his back yard? What if he couldn't guess the password and they went ahead and started the club without him? "Uh, club!" he shouted with confidence.

"Bzzt! One more wrong answer and a trap door will open and you'll fall into the moat!"

Damon jumped back, even though he now knew it was a joke. Sami laughed and so did the other person behind the gate. A girl's laugh.

Sami thrust the gate open. "Oh, Damon, you take yourself so seriously. Now get in here!"

Damon could take a joke as much as anyone, even though the reason for their meeting was deadly serious. He half grinned as he passed through the gate, where he saw the other girl. About his age, with dark hair cut into a bob—at least it looked like a bob. She was covered from head to toe in a Mexican-style blanket with alternating colors of red, yellow and orange. Her skin was impossibly smooth, and obsidian eyes sat atop a teardrop-shaped face that smiled politely, almost humbly at him. She seemed as if she was hiding from something, and, for a moment, Damon thought it was him.

Sami made the introductions. "Damon Neumeyer, this is Kierra Santorro."

Damon offered his hand. Kierra seemed reluctant to take it, but she thrust out a hand from her blanket, did a quick shake of Damon's hand, and then retracted.

"So, what's your power?" Damon asked, trying to ease the tension.

Kierra glanced at the sky. "You'll find out soon enough." Her voice was warm, and Damon didn't feel she was being rude even though her words suggested otherwise.

"Hey, guys!" Eddie called from somewhere far off. "Over here, by the pool!"

Damon turned to Sami. "Pool? Must be some kind of kiddie pool, right?" Maybe Eddie had a kid sister or brother.

Sami grinned and for probably the first time in her life said nothing. She continued to wear that grin as she marched past Damon, who followed her and Kierra as they rounded the side of the house into the back yard. A large palm tree overlooked the largest pool he had ever seen. It was set in concrete, like the pools on TV, with a silver railing and steps leading down on one end. At the opposite end perched a diving board. *A diving board?* Damon had always imagined what it would be like to dive off of a high diving board. This one was barely a few feet off the surface of the pool, but it would suffice. Damon felt an overwhelming desire to run up to the board, bounce off of it, and dive into the crystal-clear water.

"Look alive!" a nonhuman voice growled. Damon glanced up as something brown and hairy leaped at him. Two paws struck him in the chest and pushed him. As he fell, he rolled. It was Eddie. It had to be Eddie, but what was he doing? What Eddie had said earlier nagged at the back of Damon's mind. Doc Stone was afraid he couldn't control his power in full werewolf mode.

Damon rolled up to a crouching position and came face to face with the werewolf. It was much different than he remembered. The Eddie he had encountered a few years ago looked almost cuddly with neatly trimmed fur and a small snout and fangs. Hunched before him was a mature wolf with large ears, snout, and fangs twice the size of any Damon had ever seen. The fur appeared wild, as if it had never been trimmed.

"E-Eddie?"

Damon's query was met with a roar.

Instinctively, Damon exhaled. The dark space came almost at once, covering him and the werewolf. In black and white, Damon could see the beast's momentary confusion. Damon had to make his way to the house. Maybe Eddie's parents would be home and they would know what to do. But before he could make a move, the werewolf sniffed and then looked in Damon's direction.

"I smell you," the nonhuman voice growled.

The werewolf leaned forward, pounced, and landed on top of Damon. The giant maw opened, and a long tongue protruded and licked Damon in the face.

"Welcome to my home, D!" The nonhuman voice growled and then laughed. Eddie reared up and howled. Eddie had already started to revert to human form when he extended a hand to help Damon up. Damon accepted the hand, not sure what else to do. He was relieved that his new friend wasn't going to eat him, but he was also angry to be the victim of another practical joke. Almost reluctantly, he inhaled to make the dark space go away.

Sami and Kierra stood a few feet away.

"What did I miss? What did I miss?" Sami demanded.

"You should've seen him!" Eddie roared. He was now mostly human again, and his voice was that of a 15-year-old boy with only a hint of a growl. "D was scared out of his mind!"

"I was not," Damon said, even though he was.

"So, that's what you can do, Damon?" Kierra asked. "Create darkness?"

Damon nodded.

She nodded back, as if the information would somehow prove useful to her.

"I hope you don't mind, D," Eddie said. He was now mostly human except for long hairs shedding off his torso and back. For the first time, Damon noticed he was wearing sweat pants and nothing else. He hadn't noticed if the werewolf was wearing sweatpants, but he must have been, or Eddie would be naked. "This is the first time I've been able to invite friends over since they opened up the Forbidden Neighborhood, and I wanted to have fun!"

"No, I don't mind," Damon said, though he did. "So, are we going to get this meeting started?"

~ * ~

"You didn't tell me you were rich."

Damon didn't mean it to sound like an accusation. As he sat by the pool under the umbrella at a round table made of rose-tinted glass, he couldn't help feeling he'd been thrust into someone's fantasy world. Now that he was close to the pool, however, he could see the palm tree hanging over it was fake.

"You didn't ask." Eddie, sitting next to Damon, smiled a broad smile as if to say, "I have secrets you couldn't even guess." Next to him sat Sami, munching on the pepperoni slider she had picked up from Eddie's kitchen. Damon hadn't expected to be served food! This was nothing like the old Power Club meetings. He stared at the slider and cola in front of him, half expecting them to evaporate like a dream if he touched them.

Kierra completed the circle. She had grabbed the seat to Damon's right where the umbrella was tilted enough to completely hide her from the sun, which had started to peek through the cloud. "So, if you're rich," she said, cradling a can of strawberry lemonade, "your parents could have bought your way out of the district."

"They almost did," Eddie replied, "but I wanted to come."

"You wanted to live in the district?" asked Sami, almost choking on her slider. "Why would anyone want to do that?"

Eddie fingered his empty plate. He had devoured his slider in what seemed to Damon like a bite and a half. "I'd just started the fourth grade when I started to change. My teeth grew into fangs. My hair grew. I started to develop claws. Everyone knew what it was: a power. My dad owns one of the biggest construction companies in the state, so he could easily have bought my way out of the district and hired someone to come to my home and train me. But I didn't know how far it would go then, you see. How far I would change, or if I could control my power. I wanted to be around other kids so I could learn to use my power, so I wouldn't have to hide away like a lot of powered kids do until they turn eighteen and have to go through the null operation."

Damon and Sami winced at the mention of the null operation. Powered kids could have this operation when they turned eighteen. It removed their powers and allowed them to leave the district, but there were rumors that the kids were never the same afterwards.

"So, your parents moved to the district with you?" Kierra asked. "That's sweet."

"They had no choice," Eddie admitted. "The government has this idea that families should stay together. But Mom and Dad keep another residence in South Gate. That's where they are now. I have a chauffeur and a maid to look after me." He chugged his cola. "Life is sweet."

Damon tried not to seem ignorant. He never knew that powered kids' families could buy their way out of moving to the district. Miss Vogel had lived outside the district. It seemed that a lot of people with powers lived elsewhere.

Then there was Eddie himself and the matter-of-fact way in which he said he chose to live in the district. It was the right thing to do, the mature thing to do. But no kid would ever choose to live in the district. Damon was sure of it. Maybe Eddie was lying.

But some things did add up. If powered kids lived outside the district, it made sense that they would have to have the null operation at some point. Live inside the district or live outside the district, you were trapped either way. Just because you had a power you didn't ask for or even want. The idea made Damon shudder.

"You cold, D?" asked Eddie.

"I'm good," he replied. He searched for some way to get this meeting started, to direct everyone's attention back to the secret club and Calvin, but, in light of what Eddie had just told them, the idea of forming a hero club to go after a bad kid seemed lame. There was so much going on outside the district that Damon didn't know about. Finally, he turned to Kierra. "What about you? Are you going to tell us what your power is?"

Kierra huddled in her Mexican blanket, as if she were trying to make herself as small as possible. "I've been waiting for the right moment," she answered. The back of Damon's neck and shoulders warmed up, and the entire patio brightened as the sun emerged fully from the clouds. "This is it," Kierra continued. She scooted her chair back and started to rise, "By the way, Damon, that dark cloud you can make?"

"Dark space."

"Whatever. I may need your help in a few seconds. But right now I need everyone to turn away or close your eyes."

It seemed like an odd request, but Damon did as instructed. He turned away and looked past Eddie, his attention fixated on the high fence and a back gate he hadn't noticed before. Eddie and Sami shut their eyes. Damon listened carefully as Kierra's floppies trotted across the patio several feet away, then he heard the rustle of her blanket as she removed it.

Everything turned white.

Eddie, the fence, the gate, Sami, the table, the sky *glared*. And it didn't just glare. It became painful for Damon to keep his eyes open. He shut them. "What's happening?"

"Just give her a moment," Sami urged.

Eyes still shut, Damon turned in Kierra's direction, but the glare was so powerful, he could see it through his eyelids, and then it softened and flickered like a candle.

"Okay, you guys can open your eyes," Kierra announced.

Damon opened his eyes and blinked several times.

The girl covered in the Mexican blanket was gone. In her place stood something that looked like a living diamond surrounded by a glare emanating from all sides. She looked like a blue zirconium lit by Fourth of July sparklers. Damon had never seen anything so radiant, so beautiful.

"I reflect light," Kierra explained. "I learned I had this power just six months ago, but I can't control it very well. That's why I have to stay covered up." There was tension in her voice, and Damon strained to see her face. She looked like a blue film negative, but Damon could see her furrowed brow and clenched teeth. "That's also why most of my classes are at night."

"That's where I know her from," Sami chimed in. "We're in the astronomy club."

"Astronomy club?" Damon repeated. "Why does our school have an astronomy club, a theatre, and a football field? Why do you think the district goes to such great lengths to give us an 'ordinary life'?" He used air quotes. It seemed like the perfect segue into their purpose for meeting: the secret club, things going on no one knew about, Calvin.

"Hey, Damon," Kierra called out, "before we talk about that, this is where I need your help." Her voice trembled. "To use my power, all I have to do is be exposed to light. But shutting it off is trickier. Can you—?"

"You want me to create a dark space?"

He wasn't sure, but he thought he saw Kierra nod. He turned to Sami and Eddie for confirmation.

"Go!" Sami shouted.

Damon felt like a dunce for having to be prodded. He rose and slowly approached the glare. It wasn't just light. There appeared to be something solid. Every step he took became harder as the resistance increased. When he was close enough, he exhaled. A cloud of darkness covered him and Kierra. She took several deep breaths, and the glare flickered and disappeared. She picked up her blanket from the patio and wrapped herself.

"Thanks," she beamed.

"Don't mention it," Damon said in a low tone, unsure if she heard him. It didn't matter. He was so amazed by what he had just seen, he couldn't think straight. Finally, he inhaled, dispelling the dark space, and they returned to their seats. "So, Kierra, why do you want to join our club?"

She popped a bite of her slider into her mouth and chewed quickly before speaking. "I want to learn to control my power. Sami said you might be able to help."

Damon glanced at Sami, who looked embarrassed. Damon wasn't used to getting compliments from Sami.

"Beyond that," Kierra continued, "she didn't tell me much. Why do you want to start a club now that special clubs no longer exist?"

Damon took a deep breath. He couldn't have asked for a better opening. He stood and placed his hands on the back of the chair like he'd seen people on TV do when they gave a speech or said something serious. "I'm going to tell you about the purpose of this club," he began, "but first I want you to promise that nothing I say goes beyond this back yard. I need to swear you to secrecy."

"Depends on what you tell us," came a voice from behind him.

Damon whirled around. The gate at the back of the patio swung shut as a towering figure in a football jersey and a tow-headed shock of hair approached.

It was Gareth Sanderson.

Chapter Ten
Gareth's Story

Gareth had puffed himself up to twice Damon's size, so he filled out his football jersey without a shoulder harness. His muscles rippled as he strode toward Damon, who stood his ground. He had beaten Gareth once, he could do it again.

"What are you doing here?"

"I was invited." Gareth bumped Damon in the shoulder as he passed, nearly knocking him off his feet.

Damon turned to Eddie.

"He's the guy I told you about," said Eddie, watching carefully. "The guy I said would want to join the club."

"No! No way!" Damon shouted.

Gareth turned to face Damon. "I didn't know it was all up to you."

"I think we could use somebody with all those muscles," offered Sami, "if you're as strong as you look."

Non-phased, Gareth walked over to a space between Kierra and Sami and bent down. "Hold still," he told them. He grabbed their chairs by the lower arm supports and lifted. Sami shrieked. Kierra held onto one arm of her chair with both hands. Both girls looked terrified, but their terror eased as Gareth gently rocked the chairs, showing he wasn't about to drop them.

Gareth took a step back and turned around. He grinned up at the girls, showing he wasn't straining at all. Sami laughed, the nervous laugh of someone who was riding a roller coaster for the first time. Kierra bent her legs underneath the chair and lowered her head, trying to cover herself as much as she could.

"Please," she said, "the sun."

"Put her down!" Damon ordered. Helping Kierra a moment ago made him feel protective of her.

The patio darkened, and Damon looked up to see a cloud covering the sun.

"No, wait! It's okay." Kierra said. She straightened up and smiled a wide-open smile at Gareth. "You're really strong!"

"What, this?" Gareth replied. "This is nothing."

Damon fumed. Sure, it was an impressive display, but Gareth had crashed *his* meeting. Worse, he was flirting with Kierra.

Gareth completed his circle and then, like a gentleman, bent down on one knee and sat the girls back in their places. Sami burst into applause. Gareth stood up and stared Damon straight in the face, challenging him. "Wanna make something of it?"

Damon turned to Eddie. "First day of school, he knocked me down in the hall."

"Correction," Gareth interrupted. "You ran into me. You knocked yourself down."

"You picked me up and lifted me over your head! Miss Vogel had to tell you to put me down."

Gareth shrugged. "So? You always let teachers fight your battles?" Sami snickered.

"What about in the restroom? You were beating up another kid."

Gareth's demeanor changed. His easy-going smirk turned into a hard and bitter stare. He looked like he might walk right through the table and strangle Damon. "That was no kid. That was..." He stopped. "Just forget it. If you don't want me here, I don't have to be here!" He turned and stomped toward the gate.

Eddie jumped out of his chair and ran after him. They huddled by the gate and spoke in hushed tones. Damon strained to hear what they were saying. All he could make out was Eddie saying, "Tell them the whole story." They returned to the table.

"That was no kid." Gareth spoke in a low tone. "I figure he's about 22 or 23. He used to live in the Forbidden Neighborhood, just like Eddie and me. His name's Lionel Viouet."

"What's a 22 or 23-year-old doing in school?" Sami inquired.

"Picking up kids."

Sami's jaw dropped.

Damon wasn't sure he heard correctly. "You mean he's a...a ..." He wasn't even sure of the right word.

"A perv."

The word lingered in the air like the smell of rotted food. Damon shook his head. He'd heard news reports of such people outside the district, but never in the district. For all its secrecy and control, the district always seemed like a safe place...safe at least from the problems of the outside world. All Damon had had to worry about before were bullies with powers. He still couldn't comprehend exactly what a perv would do, let alone a perv with powers.

"I recognized him when I first saw him," Gareth continued. "He has the same face, no matter who or what he changes into. I saw him lure another kid into the boy's room, so I followed them in, told the other kid to beat it, and then laid into him. Then *you,*" he pointed to Damon, "you interfered. You let the perv get away."

All eyes were on Damon. He wanted to shrink and disappear between the cracks of the patio.

"I ... I didn't know," he said by way of apology.

"Wait a minute," Sami interjected. "How do you even know this Lionel Vee...Vye...?"

"Vee-you-ay," Eddie corrected her.

"Whatever. How do you know this guy in the first place?"

"Because one of his victims was my brother," Gareth answered. "Scotty was ten when Lionel lured him into his house with a piece of candy. But one of the neighbors saw him go in and told me. Eddie and I broke into Lionel's house and found Scotty. But Lionel got away."

Damon didn't want to ask, but he had to know. "Did you get your brother before...before anything happened?"

Gareth glared at Damon, resenting the question. "Scotty lived. When the police raided the house, they found—"

"Okay, stop. Stop!" Kierra waved her hand. She looked like she might throw up. "I only came here because I thought I might learn to control my power, but this is getting way too heavy for me. Damon, what does this have to do with the club you want to start?"

Damon's entire body had grown numb. The boy he had stopped Gareth from beating up, the shape shifter who could be a tree or a bird, and the perv who abused Gareth's brother were the same person, and this person was somehow in league with Calvin. Damon barely heard his own voice as he answered.

"Everything."

~ * ~

Hey Denise.

Hi, Damon.

U said u were coming to the meeting??

I had to babysit the twins. Sorry. Mom and Dad went to a counseling session with Vee.

Counseling session?

I don't want to talk about it in a chat. Maybe at school tomorrow. How did the meeting go?

Damon filled her in on who attended and what their powers were. He asked her if she'd had another vision about Calvin and what was to come.

I think so...did you say Eddie Costa attended?

Yeah. It was at his house like I told u.

He felt annoyed at having to remind her of their previous conversation.

I had a vision of something that could be a werewolf. Damon, don't trust him too much.

Damon wasn't sure he could trust any of them—but Eddie was the one he felt most comfortable around, the one who saved him in the Forbidden Neighborhood so long ago. Denise's words stung him to the core. There was so much about Eddie that surprised Damon. He was rich. He chose to live in the district. And Eddie knew Gareth, who had forced his way into the club. Damon felt sorry for Gareth's brother, but he still wasn't sure about Gareth himself. It seemed like things were getting out of his control.

Chapter Eleven
A Big Problem

Damon stood in front of the quad, carefully eyeing everything to make sure there weren't any new trees or bushes or walls or anything that might be Lionel Viouet. An increasing sense of irritation bothered him. He couldn't remember the dream exactly, but he remembered the gist of it. Denise wore a Safety Patrol jacket. She was working with Danner and Ali, who were working with Calvin. The secret club was all a ruse, they told Damon, to keep him busy and out of the way. Calvin had important work to do, and they didn't want to hurt Damon's feelings.

The last part bothered him the most. It made no sense, but it was a dream. It bothered him on the bus ride. He barely spoke to Eddie in math class, and didn't have much to say at lunch, either. Eddie and Sami didn't seem to notice. They were busy discussing their plans for the Secret Club (now its official name, they decided). Damon learned that Kierra had decided to join, though Sami suspected she just had a crush on Gareth. Damon couldn't keep his mind on the conversation. He kept sneaking glances at Eddie, to see if there was any sign he couldn't be trusted, but he had no clue what such a sign might look like. He had to talk to Denise.

A cool breeze whipped through his hair, and he daydreamed he was somewhere else—a grassy Swiss field, maybe. He heard the *cling-cling* of a bicycle bell and turned to see Denise riding toward him on a pink bike. She stopped in front of him. "Get on."

Damon regarded the pink bike and tried not to laugh.

"Are you serious?"

Her deadpan expression told him she was.

~ * ~

They rode in silence up the hill overlooking the football field.

"I wanted to make sure there was nothing or no one around that could be your Tree boy," Denise said as she dismounted.

Damon shook his legs and walked around to get rid of the cramp which had built up while he was riding. "He's not my Tree boy, his name's Lionel." He didn't want to stumble through pronouncing the last name.

"Whatever." She rocked back and forth on her heel and gathered her thoughts before continuing. "I've had another vision. Nothing clear or distinct. But I know Calvin's up to something. It's big. It's much bigger than this school or even getting revenge on us. Damon, I think he wants to start a war."

"A war?"

"A war with ords."

The idea seemed silly beyond recognition. "Calvin's family are ords, just like our families. Why would he want to start a war with them?"

"Maybe he had an unhappy childhood."

Damon laughed, but Denise cut him off with a stare. She was serious. Almost too serious. Damon remembered his dream. "Have you...talked to Danner or Ali?"

She looked confused. "No. Why would I?" There was an edge in her voice, as if it still hurt that they had rejected her.

Damon changed the subject. "What about Eddie? You said I shouldn't trust him."

She shrugged. "I don't know anything more. Like I said, I saw an animal fighting beside Calvin. It could have been a werewolf."

"Who were they fighting?"

"Us."

"Us? As in the Power Club?"

Denise nodded.

Her confirmation sent Damon into a tailspin of emotions. He wanted, more than he would ever admit, for the Power Club to start up again. Even though they had their differences, he wanted Danner involved. And Ali and Denise and even Kyle, somehow. He wanted his family back. Then he remembered something else Denise had said.

"What did you mean about Vee going to counseling?"

She folded her arms and looked away. "I didn't tell him about the robbery at Anilora's, but he found out about it later. He blames you, Damon. He thinks you didn't want him there."

"That's stupid!" Damon shouted. "With his super-speed, he could've knocked both robbers out in one second flat!"

Denise waved her hands to calm him down. "I know, but I didn't tell him that I had a vision of the robbery. And I didn't tell him that I told you about it. So, he thinks..." She swallowed. "He's been acting out ever since. He says he started the Power Club, and then you took it over. He says it would've gone the other way if he'd been there."

There was no doubt in Damon's mind that it would have. The robbers would have been stopped. Kyle wouldn't have lost his power. Maybe the Power Club would have somehow stayed together. And now Vee was blaming it all on him. "Tell him, Denise. You've got to tell him."

Her eyes flashed fear but also something else. She looked genuinely sorry. "I will. But we have to deal with this first."

Damon didn't have to ask what "this" meant. If Calvin wanted to start a war, as ridiculous as it sounded, it was all too big for Damon to grasp. His new club had just gotten started. They barely knew each other and had never done anything, let alone stop a war. And how did the Power Club fit into all this? Was Denise even telling the truth? She had lied to her brother, and she had lied in the dream.

Maybe if Denise came to the next meeting, she could tell the others about her visions, and they could ask more questions—questions Damon couldn't think of. Maybe they could all work up some kind of plan. Damon didn't know why he thought that. He just didn't want to try to figure it out by himself.

He told Denise about the next meeting. She agreed to come.

~ * ~

Damon didn't want to go to the next meeting. It had been a busy and exhausting day, full of classes that went on forever. He wanted to tell someone, any adult, what he'd learned, but he couldn't chance it. Keeping a secret while trying to focus on polynomials, the Dred Scott Decision, and sprinting around the school's race track took its toll. All he wanted to do was go home and sleep until next year.

But go to the meeting he did. They were all there—Eddie, Sami, Kierra, and even Gareth. Damon was starting to warm up to the idea of having a strong man on the team, especially one who had a reason to go after Tree boy. Now, all they had to do was wait for Denise.

After twenty minutes of chit chat and eating leftover sliders, the others grew restless.

"Why don't you call this girl?" Eddie asked.

It was a test, Damon figured, to see if he had her number. Then they could tease him about having a girlfriend. That's what the other boys in his class would do. But Damon had an out.

"I don't have a phone," he admitted.

"Then what's her number?" Eddie whipped out his phone—the latest model.

"I don't know. I've only been able to contact her through the chat on my computer at home." It sounded like a lame excuse, even as he said it. As the club's leader, he should have her number. He should have all their numbers.

"Well, I'm not sitting around waiting!" Gareth bolted out of his chair as if he had been forced to sit too long. Damon thought he might leave. But Gareth went to the other end of the pool and put on another show of strength by hoisting the fake palm tree over his head.

"Ooh, I've got an idea!" Kierra jumped out of her chair and stretched her hand toward the palm tree. She looked up at the sky, as if waiting for a cue. Heavy clouds blanketed the sky, so there was no danger of her losing control of her power like she had yesterday, she told them, but enough of the sun peaked through to allow her to do "weird things." She manipulated her fingers as if she were controlling atoms. The palm tree lit up like a glitter prop from Las Vegas.

"Whoah!" Gareth shouted and thrust the blazing palm tree toward the pool.

"Not in the pool!" Eddie yelled.

Gareth looked for someplace else to toss the luminous object, but then he squinted at it and relaxed. "Hey, it's not hot."

"No." Kierra sounded disappointed. "I can only reflect light, not heat."

"That's still amazing!" Eddie shouted.

Kierra blushed.

Even Damon was caught up in the display. There was so much about these kids and their powers he still needed to know—and they needed to know what he could do. He would have to forget about Denise. She would either come or she wouldn't. Maybe she had to babysit again.

~ * ~

Night started to fall when Damon crossed the boulevard back into his own neighborhood. He no longer felt exhausted. He felt energized. The new club was a real thing. It could actually happen. Maybe they had a chance against Calvin. There were some rough spots, of course. Sami spent most of the evening sulking because her enhanced hearing wasn't of much use during most maneuvers, unless somebody tried to sneak up on her. She tried to compensate by being bossy, but she stopped when Gareth nicknamed her "Lucy," after the *Peanuts* character.

Damon suppressed a smile that someone's power was less flashy than his own. His dark space had its uses, but it couldn't hold a candle— literally or figuratively—to what Kierra, Gareth, and Eddie could do. Their powers were made for going up against villains. Damon wasn't sure his was. He demonstrated how he could expand and contract the dark space and create sound spaces so others could hear. Gareth waved his hand and said, "That's nothing."

But Damon wasn't going to let his opinion get the best of him. There were too many other things to think about, to plan for. As he climbed the sidewalk of his own block Damon barely noticed as something large moved toward him.

"HEY, YOU!" a voice boomed.

Damon looked up. Danner Young peered down at him. A thirty-foot-tall Danner Young. Through a pair of trees.

Chapter Twelve
Rallying the Troops

Danner pushed his way through the trees and advanced. Damon stepped back. The giant didn't look like he was paying a friendly visit.

He wore his Safety Patrol jacket, which, like the rest of his clothes, grew or shrunk with him. As Danner shrunk, Damon saw he was carrying something. Another jacket.

"I-Is that for me?" Damon couldn't hide the thrill in his voice. Was Danner truly bringing him is own Safety Patrol jacket? Did he reconsider and decide to ask Damon to join, after all? What would Damon tell the Secret Club?

Danner held the jacket up. "Does this look like something that belongs to you?" In the twilight, Damon squinted to read the name emblazoned in red. Ali's name.

"Why are you showing me Ali's jacket?"

"Don't play stupid with me." Danner clenched his fists. "What have you done with her?"

More confused than ever, Damon said, "Nothing."

The six-foot Danner howled in rage and lunged at Damon. Before Damon could react, the older boy grabbed him by the shirt and hoisted him off the ground.

"If you release a dark space, I'll pound your ass. And I'm holding onto you so you don't make me disappear, too. Now, for the last time. WHERE. IS. ALI?"

Damon tried to remain calm, but his heart pounded as hard as he imagined a beating from Danner's oversized fists would feel. "Danner, I didn't send Ali anywhere. My power can't do that. Like I told you, that was just a lie the district made up about me. Besides, I've been with friends all evening."

Danner's eyes narrowed. "A twerp like you has friends? Who?"

Damon started to speak, then stopped. The Secret Club was supposed to be secret.

"That's what I thought!" Danner spat as he spoke, and Damon winced at the unwelcome shower. "I'm going to tell you this only once. Bring her back. Now."

"I-I can't. Besides, how do you know she disappeared? Maybe she dropped her jacket." Damon spoke fast, stalling for time.

Danner shook his head. "She wouldn't do that. We were working out in the quad with Rusty and a couple of other guys. Afterwards, we decided to go for pizza. Ali said she had to get something from her locker and she'd meet us, but she never showed. I went back to the quad and found her jacket. Her phone's still in her pocket. That means I can't call her. That means something's happened to her. That means you did something."

Damon knew it was pointless to argue with his logic. Worse, if Danner's account was true, Damon had a feeling he knew what happened.

"Danner, listen to me," he said, lowering his voice and speaking as clearly and calmly as he could. "If Ali's disappeared, I think I know who's responsible. Denise told me about a vision—"

The massive arms thrust Damon backwards, and his back and the back of his head collided with a tree. The jolt stunned him.

"No lies!" Danner shouted. He grabbed Damon by the shirt again and pushed him away from the tree. Damon's feet tripped over each other as he tried to stay upright. "The rest of the Safety Patrol is out looking for you, too! I'm gonna take you to Doc Stone, and he'll call the police. They'll get the truth outta you!"

The police? If the police got hold of him, Damon figured, he'd be a sitting duck for Calvin. Last year, the police couldn't hold Calvin. That's how he got away.

It was a risky move, but he saw no choice. He spied a tree stump just ahead of him, staggered toward it, and tripped over it. He held his arm close to his chest so it wouldn't hurt when he landed and hoped Danner wouldn't notice.

Damon rolled over in the grass, clutching his arm, and cried out.

Danner stopped. "You okay?"

Damon exhaled, and the inky blackness of the dark space spread forward like a cloud of nothing, covering him and Danner. It was a dirty trick, but it worked.

As his night vision activated, Damon saw everything in pristine black and white. Danner looked disoriented and scared. Damon imagined what he was thinking. *He thinks I've sent him someplace, like Ali.* Damon scrambled to his feet and stepped slightly to one side, away from the place Danner had last seen him. Then he concentrated and opened a sound space.

"Take it easy, Danner. You're still on earth." Damon's voice had a cocky swagger, like someone who had just gained the upper hand. But that cockiness disappeared, as Danner swung a fist in Damon's direction. Damon barely ducked in time to avoid being hit. *Stupid! He can tell the direction of my voice.*

Damon considered running around Danner, but that wouldn't do. Sooner or later, he'd figure out where Damon was. Somehow, he had to keep Danner from guessing where he was. Then it hit him. A year ago, Damon had figured out how to create more than one dark space at the same time—multiple layers, like layers of frosting on a chocolate cake. He hadn't attempted to do it since his power recovered from the null grenade, but he thought maybe he could do something else. He concentrated.

The dark space tightened and wobbled. *It's resisting me.* Damon used to think the dark space was alive, like a mysterious friend or pet. Whatever it was, it occasionally seemed to be aware—and, like an animal, it resisted doing things it did not understand. *It's okay. Trust me. We can do this.* The inky cloud relaxed, and a second sound space opened.

Damon carefully coaxed the second sound space a few feet away from the first before he spoke.

"Listen, Danner."

Damon and Danner both jumped. His voice sounded like it came from a loudspeaker.

"Whoa!" Damon grinned.

Danner looked around, although he couldn't see anything, trying to figure out where the voice was coming from.

"I know you don't believe me, but I didn't send Ali away. I

couldn't. Besides, I wouldn't. She's my friend, too."

Danner grunted and took a swipe at Damon, missing him completely.

"But I think I know who did. You remember Calvin? The kid who sent me into the orange dimension? Well, Denise says he's back and he wants to start a war."

Danner took another swipe in the opposite direction. "Kids don't start wars! Besides, the police sent him away to Alaska."

"That was a lie, just like the lie about my power sending people away. Calvin escaped."

"Yeah? How do you know?"

"I can't tell you." Damon still felt bound to the promise he made to the man and woman at the hospital.

"Then how do I know you're not lying?"

Damon couldn't think of an answer.

"Look, Danner, all I know is, if I had the power to send Ali away, I could send you away too, but I haven't. Why do you think that is?"

Danner stopped swinging.

"You know I can just grow taller and walk out of your ridiculous dark space."

"It's not—" Damon stopped himself. Defending his power against an insult seemed less important than something he realized. "So, why haven't you?"

"Because," Danner swayed back and forth as if wrestling with something inside him, "part of me wants to believe you're telling the truth. You did a lot of good last year, at the mall and Anilora's. But I need you to give me a sign of trust. Drop your dark space."

It was a trap. It had to be. Danner had learned a lot of fighting techniques from his dad, a district police officer. Maybe he'd also learned how to talk people off a ledge. That's how Damon felt: like he was on a ledge and about to plunge into the abyss.

"I'll drop it," he said, "but before I do, promise me something. Before you take me to Doc Stone, call Denise. She'll confirm everything I just said."

Danner nodded.

~ * ~

Damon fidgeted while Danner called Denise. Her phone went to voicemail. Nothing unusual in that, but it made Damon worry what Danner would do next. Danner punched in another number. "I'm calling her dad," he explained. "I used to work in his auto shop and still have his number."

An intense moment later, Mr. Evans answered. The conversation was clipped and short. Danner hung up, looking serious. "He said Denise didn't come home from school. Neither did Vee. The district police told Mr. and Mrs. Evans to keep the line open and only tell people who need to know." He cocked his head back. "Probably a simple explanation. Kids don't always come home from school. Maybe they went to a party."

"Together?" Damon asked. It would be strange for a high school freshman to go to a party with her seventh-grade brother.

Danner punched the auto-dial and raised the phone to his ear. "Doc Stone? Yeah, listen...yeah, I found him." He glanced at Damon. "I don't think that's a good idea, sir. One of my other friends has also disappeared. Denise..."

Damon tried to pick up the gist of the conversation, but it was hard since Danner did more listening than talking and was reduced to the occasional grunt. Finally, Danner grunted "okay, bye," and hung up.

"Doc says not to worry about it," he announced with confidence. "He says the district has things under control, and they will find Denise and Vee. Meanwhile, he says you ought to go home, but tomorrow he wants you to report to him first thing when you get to school."

Damon didn't like the sound of that. He was grateful for the reprieve of the Safety Patrol letting him go home tonight. Maybe that would give him time to think, to do...something. But why did Doc Stone even want to see him? Did the Safety Patrol's advisor still think he had something to do with Ali's disappearance, and now Denise's and...

"Wait a minute," Damon said, "how did he know about Vee?"

"What do you mean?"

"He said Denise and Vee would be fine, but you only mentioned

Denise."

Danner looked past Damon, as if he were staring into some invisible tunnel that might contain the answer. "Maybe...he has contacts at the district."

"But Mr. Evans said they were telling only people who need to know. Why would a high school club advisor need to know?"

Danner couldn't answer. He stared at Damon, and, for half a second, Damon felt Danner's world collapsing around him. The sensation rocked Damon. It was his world, too.

~ * ~

Damon ran up the block as fast as he could. It was urgent that he get home and make a few calls. *Damn it, Mom! I wouldn't have to do this if I had my own phone.* Not only would having his own phone mean he could have already made those calls, but he wouldn't have to go home and face his mother and explain everything.

He'd be grounded, for sure.

Danner went home, too. When you're a twenty-foot giant, you can get home quicker. They should have stayed together, Damon argued, but Danner wanted to go home and check something with his father. It wasn't safe, he said, to call him on the phone. Damon didn't know if Danner knew it wasn't safe or if he was just guessing, but he didn't ask. Their uneasy truce might fall apart with too many questions.

It was dark by the time Damon reached the front porch. He wanted to barge inside and head for the landline, but his mother would ask questions if he came in all out of breath. He couldn't afford the questions. Or the time. He bent over panting. Finally, he was able to breathe normally. He would just pretend everything was normal as he made his way into the kitchen, where the landline awaited.

"I was about to call the police," Damon's mother said as he entered the living room. The yellow light from the table lamp illuminated the room with a sickly, dull hue as Leah Neumeyer reclined on the couch, her attention focused on a nighttime soap opera and only briefly interrupted by her son's entrance.

"What?" Damon said, wondering how she could have known.

"You said you'd be home an hour ago."

"Oh." Damon felt the weight of doom lift from him. "Meeting ran long. Sorry."

"How did your meeting with your new friends go?"

"Fine." Damon started for the kitchen.

"Your old friend Danner stopped by and asked for you. I hope it's okay, but I told him where you'd gone."

So, that's how he knew where to find me. "He's not my f—" The word caught in Damon's throat. Maybe it wasn't true anymore. Maybe he and Danner were friends now. Or allies, at least. "I need to make a call."

Leah Neumeyer took a sip from the beer can which had been resting on the table and turned her attention back to the soap opera. Damon thought he saw her nod, but whether it was to acknowledge his statement or because of something on TV he couldn't tell.

Although Damon wasn't allowed to have his own phone, his mother kept a landline affixed to a wall in the kitchen. It was an antique—a rotary phone with numbers you actually dialed. *Who had those anymore?* Leah said it belonged to her parents and was one of the few things she kept when she moved her family to the district—a requirement once Damon developed a power. Every time Damon saw the phone, he thought it was just there to remind him it was his fault for uprooting their lives! He scrupulously avoided the phone—there was no one he wanted to call anyway. But tonight the phone might save a few lives. He lifted the headset off its cradle and pulled from his jeans pocket a scrap of paper on which he had scrawled four phone numbers.

He thought he should call Eddie first, but something tugged at the back of his mind. Denise's vision. Was Eddie secretly working with Calvin? No. Damon wouldn't believe it. But, just in case, he dialed Gareth's number first. But there was no answer. The phone didn't even go to voicemail.

He dialed Sami's number.

"You know who you are," the voicemail began. "You know who I am. Leave a message."

Typical.

74

"Hey, Sami, this is Damon. If you get this message soon, call me back. It's urg—"

Sami's voice—her real voice—interrupted. "Hey, Damon, what's up?" She sounded drowsy.

Damon explained the situation as best he could and that it was time for the Secret Club to go after Calvin.

There was a pause. "Damon, it's the middle of the night."

Damon glanced at the digital clock on the wall. "It's only nine."

"Look." She dragged out the word as if she were thinking of an excuse. "This Secret Club has been fun, but you're seriously saying we should go after a kid who can make people disappear!"

Damon wasn't sure what to say. "But I thought you wanted to get back at Calvin for what he did to Suzy Steele."

"I do," she asserted. "But when we were working out today, it made me realize just how little I have to contribute. I mean, super-hearing—what's that? That's nothing compared to super-strength or turning into a werewolf. Call Gareth and Eddie."

"I'm going to call everyone!" He didn't think it wise to tell her he couldn't get a hold of Gareth. Maybe he could try again. "I'm going to call Kierra, too."

"Don't bother. She's right here. We're having a sleepover."

"Oh, well—" Damon perked up, thinking that, even if Sami didn't want to come, maybe Kierra might. But before he could ask Sami to pass the phone, he heard the two girls' voices arguing.

"Kierra says you should call the police," Sami said.

"The district police won't do anything. We've been over this. Gareth says they didn't do anything to stop Lionel Whatever from molesting his brother or other children."

"That was in the Forbidden Neighborhood, which no longer exists." Her logic was unassailable. "Besides, we don't even know where to find Calvin."

"Danner said he thinks his dad might be able to find out. He's supposed to call me." Then, an idea hit Damon. "Look, with your hearing, you can probably find Calvin before anyone else can, if Danner's dad can give us a general location. Then, all you have to do is tell us where he is, then you can leave. Okay?"

"Okay," came a terse reply. "But that's it." The arguing returned. "Kierra's coming too." More arguing. Damon thought he heard Kierra say *No! No!* "I'm not going there by myself," Sami said through clenched teeth. She then returned to the phone. "Call us back when you know where we're going." The phone disconnected.

Only Eddie's number remained. Damon stared at it like it was a secret code to a game. Either the number would lead to salvation or doom. He wished he could be sure which. But maybe Denise was wrong. She did say she only saw a monster of some kind. It could be anything. Damon dialed the number.

When Eddie answered, Damon explained the situation.

"So, it's really happening." Eddie sounded calm. "Damn. I wish we had more time to practice."

"Me, too. But if Calvin's made the others disappear, Danner and I are next. It's better to strike first."

"I guess. So, what's the plan? How do we get Calvin to bring the other kids back?"

Damon hadn't thought that far ahead. He knew Calvin wouldn't bring them back unless he wanted to. They would have to give him a reason to do so. "He doesn't want to get arrested again and sent to Alaska. Maybe the district police have found a way to keep him from escaping this time."

"That's a big *maybe.*" Eddie sounded perturbed. "Look, maybe Gareth and I can lean on him, if you know what I mean."

"I, uh, couldn't get a hold of Gareth." Damon bit his tongue as soon as he said it. *Damn honesty.*

But Eddie didn't sound upset. "I know where he lives. I'll find him. Just call me back as soon as Danner calls you."

Damon agreed and hung up. As soon as he did, the phone rang. He snatched the receiver off its cradle, hoping his mother hadn't heard it ring. "H-hello?"

"Who's been tying up your phone?" Danner screamed. "I've been trying to reach you for ten minutes."

Damon was relieved that it was Danner and not someone else—a friend of Eldon's, maybe, or Grandma Allen, who still dialed the landline on occasion. The last thing Damon wanted to do was explain to his grandmother he couldn't talk to her right now. Just the same, he resented being screamed at.

"What'd you find out, Danner?"

"According to my dad, the district police know Calvin's back. But they can't keep track of him."

Small wonder, Damon thought, with a kid who can open a rift to other dimensions and jump inside.

"Dad said Calvin's displacement signature lingers around his old neighborhood. They've been keeping his old house under surveillance, but so far they haven't spotted him."

"Wait a minute. What's a displacement signature?"

"Every time Calvin opens a rift, it displaces atoms and molecules, weakening the barrier between our world and the other dimension. There's a special device that can detect it, but the signature doesn't last long. That's why the police can't track him. They have to be nearby when he opens a rift and returns to our world."

"Then the next thing we need to do is go to Calvin's house. Maybe we can find him when the police can't."

"And just how do we do that?"

Damon smiled with pride as he told Danner about the Secret Club, which included a girl with super-hearing.

"Are you crazy? We can't bring more kids into this. This isn't some comic book, Damon. Calvin's dangerous, in case you hadn't figured that out."

"Hey, I'm the guy he sent into the orange dimension, remember?" Damon struggled not to lose his cool or raise his voice. "We need help, Danner. We can't rely on your Safety Patrol since Doc Stone may be involved somehow. The Secret Club is all we've got." There was a pause on the other end. Damon pressed his advantage. "Look, I've worked out with these guys, and they're really good. Eddie said he and Gareth could lean on Calvin, maybe make him bring back Denise and the others."

"Oh, great! You've gone from somebody reading comic books to somebody watching gangster movies! No, Damon! Just no! Christ, I don't even know these kids."

"You know Eddie," Damon countered. "He tried out for the Safety Patrol. He's the guy who can turn into a werewolf, remember?"

There was a laugh on the other end. Or a cry. Maybe both. "Listen, stupid, I don't know what this Eddie guy told you, but nobody who can turn into a werewolf has ever tried out for the Safety Patrol."

Chapter Thirteen
The House on the Hill

The cool wind whipped through Damon's hair as he rode toward Calvin's neighborhood. It was that time of year when nights got cold fast. He had never really noticed or cared before. He found himself gulping every breath—to calm his nerves, he told himself. But it was really because he thought every breath might be the last one he would ever take on this planet, the world of his birth.

His mouth contorted with disgust as an involuntary memory intruded. A thin atmosphere permeated the orange dimension where Calvin had marooned him last year. Every breath made Damon feel like he was suffocating—the air was hot and full of sand. Damon did not want to go back there. He wondered if that's where Calvin had sent Denise and the others—if he sent them anywhere.

Damon had to know the truth. He pedaled faster. The crisp night sky and brilliant street lights lit the way as he passed the old school—the only place he could remember going to school until a few days ago—-and Mackintosh Park, where he had played so much as a kid and where the Power Club had worked out. It seemed like a lifetime ago.

Passing the park, he took a right down Calvin's street. The houses were older and creepy. They stood up on hills bordered by retaining walls. Even the curbs seemed larger, as if to discourage kids from riding their bikes onto them. Damon had passed through this neighborhood several times on rides with his parents but had never gotten to see the houses up close. Most were two-story clapboards in need of fresh paint.

Calvin's house was easy to find. Most of the houses were illuminated by porch lights or security lights, but Calvin's was dark. As Damon approached, he saw a piece of wood covering a large picture window on the porch, overlooking the street. It seemed obscene. A picture window is where kids looked out at the street, where families gathered to open Christmas presents, where Mom and Dad could relax on a swing while their kids played inside. Damon always wished his own house had a picture window.

Calvin had lost so much. When he escaped, his parents lacked what the government called a "qualifying child" to remain in the district. What must it have been like for Calvin to come back and see his home this way?

I won't feel sorry for him. I won't. Calvin's the bad guy. He got what he deserved. Judging Calvin made Damon feel worse.

He rode his bike up on the curb and stopped between a row of bushes and a steep concrete stairwell. There was no sign of Danner's bike. *Maybe he just grew large and walked here.*

Damon looked around for a place to stash his bike, but only the large bushes provided cover. He found an opening and shoved his bike into it.

"OWW!" someone shrieked.

Damon jumped back, prepared for anything as the bush rustled and a figure emerged. Even in the dark, he recognized the rust-colored hair and turquoise glasses.

"Sami! What're you doing in there?"

"Spying. What else?" She pushed Damon's bike back toward him. "Stick this somewhere else."

"But how did you get here before I did?" Sami lived even further from Calvin's neighborhood.

Agitated, Sami brushed her hands and knees of dirt. "Kierra lives on the next block. That's where we were having our sleepover. I've been here for twenty minutes. I thought no one else was coming."

"Oh," Damon said, feeling bad that it had taken him so long to sneak out of the house. He'd waited until his mother had gone upstairs. Then he retrieved the garage key from the pantry so he could get his bike. He really should have asked his mother's permission to leave the house so late, but that would have led to so many questions. He would definitely be grounded when he got back, if he got back. He looked past Sami to see if anyone else was hiding in the bushes. "Where's Kierra?"

"Not coming." Sami almost spat the words. "She thinks we're crazy. Maybe she's right. What about Eddie?"

Damon told Sami what Danner had said, that Eddie had lied about trying out for the Safety Patrol. He also told her about Denise's dream about a "monster" fighting alongside Calvin.

Sami stared up at Damon, her eyes wide with disbelief. "The snake! Do you think he was using us?"

"I don't know. But I didn't call him back to tell him where we were going."

"That was smart. What about Gareth?"

"No answer."

"So, it's just the two of us?" Her voice was laced with panic.

"Danner's supposed to be here...wait, you said you'd been here twenty minutes, and you didn't see anybody else?"

She shook her head.

Damon looked around, indecisive. "Maybe Danner came in the back way," he said, pointing to Calvin's house. "That must be it. Maybe he's doing recon." It made Damon feel brave to use a word the police might use. Danner's dad was a police officer. Surely, that's what Danner was doing. Damon started up the stairs.

"Wait!" Sami tugged at his arm. "Where are you going?"

"To see if I can find him. You coming?"

Sami shook her head vigorously. "Like I said, super-hearing's not much good in a battle, if it comes to that. I can be your spy, but that's about it."

Damon nodded. He was grateful Sami had come, even if it meant he'd have to risk facing Calvin alone.

"There's something else you should know," she continued. "Calvin's in there, and he's not alone."

"Who else is with him?"

"I can't make it out, but it sounds like somebody older—an adult, maybe."

Must be Lionel Viouet—tree boy.

Sami whipped out her phone from her pants pocket. As the screen lit her face in an eerie blue, Damon heard it vibrate.

"Not now, Mr. Kytel," she said through clenched teeth as her fingers flew across the screen to shut off the phone.

"Mr. Kytel? The math teacher?"

"He's replying to a question I had over our math homework."

Damon sneered. "You keep your teachers' numbers in your phone?"

"Only their school numbers," Sami answered. She looked defensive as she saw Damon's expression. "That's how I got to be so smart!" She stuck her tongue out at him, and, for a moment, she was Sami the Snitch all over again.

"You got all your teachers' numbers?" Damon asked.

"Of course."

"Well, look, if something happens up there and I don't come back, there's somebody I want you to call."

~ * ~

Damon never wished he was an ord, even though having a power meant he had to live in the district. He always thought of his dark space as something special, something that made him special, that made him who he was. Even in a place full of powered kids, it gave him something no one else had. He'd never met another kid with a power even close to his. Still, there were times when he wished it could do more.

The dark space would be useless as he approached Calvin's house. All Damon could do was surround himself in darkness, and though his night vision allowed him to see inside the void, he could not see outside of it. What good was it to be able to see only a few steps in front of him? Tonight, he'd learned how to create more than one sound space within the void. Maybe if he continued to practice...but there was no time. He had to find Danner.

At the top of the stairs, the concrete walk split into two paths, snaking along either side of the house. To the left, the hill sloped upwards and disappeared into the next yard—the perfect spot for an ambush. Damon chose the path on the right.

The grass in the side yard rose to Damon's ankles and encroached on the path. He inched his way along the side of the house until he came to a window. Unlike the picture window on the front of the house, it wasn't boarded up. He dropped to his knees to crawl past it, but curiosity got the better of him. Slowly, he craned his neck.

The inside was dark but lit by a small light source at the far end. It was bigger than a night light but smaller than a table lamp and appeared to be sitting on the floor. The room was large and seemed to span the width of the house. He saw no furniture or even carpets, just a wooden floor. Damon imagined it had been teeming with life once. He imagined young Calvin running around playing cowboy or sprawled on the floor watching TV—things Damon and his brother did. He wondered if Calvin had a brother.

He didn't know why he kept wanting to identify with Calvin, to feel sorry for him. Damon supposed he didn't want to believe anybody could really be that bad, even though Calvin had done a lot of bad things. But to start a war with ords? How could somebody who lived in a house like this, who had a family of ords, want to do such a thing?

Further down the walk lay another window. This one belonged to the kitchen, which Damon surmised from the vacant space and electrical outlets where a refrigerator once stood. But there was more. On the counter sat more portable lights like the one he had observed in the living room. They illuminated a workspace covered in large sheets of corrugated paper. *Maps.* No wonder the police couldn't detect Calvin's presence. His operation was so low-tech that he used battery-powered lights and paper maps.

Something moved. Damon dropped to his hands and knees. For several seconds, he did not allow himself to even breathe. When nothing happened, he figured he hadn't been spotted.

Damon crawled past the window and toward the end of the house, which opened into a small backyard.

"How long we gotta wait?" said a familiar voice.

A second voice, sounding irritated, mumbled the answer.

Damon inched closer until he could see the entire backyard. At the far end, gathered around an old barrel were two figures. One took a puff of a cigarette, the light from it momentarily illuminating his face and scraggly hair. He was the one whose voice Damon recognized. Rusty Reddick.

Figures. He was Calvin's friend. And now he's a member of the Safety Patrol. I bet he's been working with Calvin all along.

The second figure stood with his back to Damon, but he recognized the six-foot frame, overbearing posture, and, most telling, the Safety Patrol jacket.

Why is Danner hanging out with Rusty in Calvin's back yard?

Maybe it was all just a joke, after all, like in Damon's dream.

Rusty spoke. "So, you're sure the house is empty?"

"Yup," Danner replied tersely.

The house is NOT empty. But why would Danner think it was? Had he searched it already? That wasn't the plan. And Danner, whatever else he did, liked to stick to plans.

Damon observed them carefully. Danner walked around the barrel and said something to Rusty. The latter nodded, crushed out his cigarette in the gravel, and thrust his hands down at this side. His hands glowed, and twin bursts of solar energy emerged, propelling Rusty into the dark sky. He arched behind some trees and vanished.

Damon's jaw dropped. He didn't know Rusty could do that. His dark space seemed even more limited.

Danner turned around from the barrel and headed to the other side of the backyard. In the brush, Damon saw a barely concealed bike. *So that's how he got here. And now he's leaving. Maybe he's decided to call off the mission. But...* They couldn't just leave! This could be their only chance of getting their friends back.

Damon rose and sprinted through the back yard, trying to make as little noise as possible "Danner!" he whispered. "Danner!" The other boy continued toward the bike. Damon ran faster, and until was close enough to grab Danner by the sleeve of his jacket. "Hey, Danner!"

The boy who turned around was not Danner. The face was older, twisted into a grin Damon had seen before—in the restroom and in the quad. Tree boy. Lionel Viouet.

"I told you to mind your own business," said the dark voice, followed by a laugh.

Damon backed away. How could he be so stupid? He turned to run, but his feet went nowhere. The ground rose up to meet him, and he caught a glimpse of Calvin, sitting atop the triangular overhang of the back porch, cackling with glee. Damon reached out, trying to grab onto anything, but the rift was too wide. There was no time to scream.

Interlude 1

...then Damon went up to Calvin's house, and he hasn't come back.

> Bummer. Have you heard anything?

A few mins ago, I heard him say Danner's name, so he must have found the other guy. The other guy said something about minding his own business, and then there was laughter.

THAT STUPID RAT!!

> Maybe it's some kind of joke.

> Why don't you just come back to my house and leave those boys and their stupid mission?

'Cause I promised. I just wish you were here.

> Me, too, but my mom would kill me if I snuck out of the house.

I know. I just feel so alone sitting here in the bush, waiting. Damon couldn't even get ahold of Gareth.

> Gareth??? He's here.

NO WAY!

> He just dropped by to see if I was
> doing anything.

ARE YOU?? 😊

> Sami! 😮 😮
> Now that he's here, I feel better
> about going
> out at night. We'll come and get you.

Great. Thx.

Sami put her phone on sleep. It was risky to use it should somebody walk by and see a glowing light emanating from the bush. But she couldn't stand the silence and the waiting. Maybe Damon forgot she was there, after all. That would be just like him.

But there was more to it. The way Damon had organized the club, the way he led everybody during their training exercise...even Gareth followed his direction. Damon knew what he was doing. He went up there to face Calvin by himself. His bravery impressed Sami, and so did his stupidity. *Oh, Damon, what have you gotten yourself into?*

She checked the display on her phone. Fifteen minutes since Damon had gone up the stairs. Fifteen minutes since she last saw him. Well, he may have forgotten her or not, but she was going to do what he asked her to do. She opened her phone directory and pressed a number.

Interlude 2

Antoinette Vogel pressed the disconnect button on her phone. As indelicate as it was to take a call in the ladies' room of the Figaro Opera House, she was glad she had. It was so rare that students called her school number that when an alert popped up on her phone, she was more than curious. However, it wasn't the kind of call she expected. The student on the other end did not ask her what tomorrow's reading assignment was or tell her she would not be in class due to illness. What Sami Andrus told her was the last thing she expected, yet the thing she had most feared.

Her boyfriend, Brandon, was annoyed at the interruption. Antoinette had excused herself in the middle of *Three-penny Opera* to answer the call. She saw his hurtful, pouty expression. *Not again.* She enjoyed Brandon's company, but he would have to understand: her students came first.

She opened the door to the ladies' room. Brandon stood guard outside, just as he had promised. In his tuxedo, he would easily be mistaken for an usher and could guide other patrons away until Antoinette completed her call. He looked back at her with that charming half smile of his.

"All okay?"

"I hate to do this," she whispered, "but I must leave." Before he could object, she quickly added, "One of my students may be in trouble. That part of the district isn't far from here, so I should just be able to pop over and check it out, but I may not be able to return before the play is over. Please don't be mad." It was a weak plea, but she really did enjoy his company. Besides, she would need his help to safeguard her jewelry, her purse—and her clothes.

"What do you want from me?" There was no hint of irritation in his voice, just a soldier's dispassionate request for orders.

"Wait five minutes, then come in and pick up my clothes. Stash them somewhere. When I return, I will find you."

~ * ~

The city lights flew by underneath her. Antoinette loved flying at night. As the cool wind whipped through her wings, she felt powerful, above it all, and far removed from the cares of powered children and terrorists and the district. In her bird form, she was blue with gold and green streaks in her feathers...beautiful by anyone's standards. She also stood out like an impossible creature: a hawk-sized peacock. She wished she could transform into something less conspicuous—a robin or a blackbird to blend in with the night—but her power didn't work that way. She just hoped she could get in and out before Calvin Goodrich or the other members of his cell spotted her.

It wasn't hard to find the address Sami gave her. Antoinette had memorized the layout of the district and the locations of most neighborhoods. Sami and three other students stood on the sidewalk in front of the house. Sami hadn't mentioned other students would be involved. She hoped they wouldn't do anything stupid.

Antoinette flew past them and circled the house. No one else was outside. There was no sign of Damon Neumeyer or Danner Young, the two students Sami had said were trying to find Calvin. Antoinette hoped they hadn't found him, had given up, and gone home. It would have been terrible to leave Sami behind, but kids had done worse.

She noticed one of the windows on the north side of the house slightly raised. She perched on the wooden windowsill and listened for any sign of movement from within. Soon enough, she heard voices.

"... I still say we should set up somewhere else." It was an adult male voice, one she recognized but couldn't place.

"No! This is my home. We're stayin'." A younger voice. Calvin, she assumed.

"But when you bring those kids back, they will know where we are."

"Who says I'm bringin' 'em back?"

"Calvin, the Liberator said—"

"Forget the Liberator!"

"Hey, Calvin," said an agitated teen voice, "you didn't say anything about sending them away forever!"

"You growin' soft on me, Rus?"

"No! It's just...I didn't sign on to kill anybody."

"I didn' say nothin' 'bout killin'? I sent them to a place wit' oxygen an' food, if they can find it. An' I sent them all to the same place, so they won' get lonesome. See? I'm a real humanitarian."

"Well, I don't care where you sent them. I just wish I could have had some fun with them before you did." Another older voice. One she recognized. One she hoped she would never hear again. "It's too hot in here," the voice continued. Footsteps approached the window. Before she could react, a leering face appeared and pushed the window up further. The movement startled her, and she took off.

She hoped he hadn't recognized her. She recognized him. He had been her neighbor. He always seemed kind, giving her and other kids candy. He always invited them in to see his movie collection. They always said no. But when his nephew started visiting and hanging out with them, some of Antoinette's friends went inside. They never returned. Only later did Antoinette learn there was no nephew. The neighbor, Mr. Viouet, was a shape changer, just like she was. She could only become a bird. But he could become anything, even a kid.

Antoinette circled the sidewalk, but Sami and the other kids had vanished. She hoped they'd gone home. She flew as fast as she could back to the Figaro Opera House. She had to reach her phone. She replayed in her mind her conversation with Sami. She had counseled Sami to call the district police. It was the teacherly thing to do. But Sami repeated what Damon had told her: The district police wouldn't do anything. And she was right.

Antoinette cursed the district. They would sacrifice kids to capture the Liberator.

When she regained her clothes and Brandon, she told him to wait in the lobby for her. The call she was about to make wasn't for his ears. Angry tears burned her cheeks as she realized she couldn't help Damon and

Danner and whoever else Calvin had sent away. But she could make sure neither Calvin nor the district got away with it.

Interlude 3

The sound of bicycles approaching startled Sami, but, when she heard voices, she recognized who they belonged to. Her elation turned to horror as she heard a third familiar voice. She popped up out of the bushes—a dangerous move, but she was too angry to care.

Kierra—her omnipresent blanket blowing in the wind—and Gareth rode in from one direction.

Eddie rode in from another.

"Stop!" she hissed as Eddie's racing bike stopped at the curb. "What are you doing here?"

"I called him," said Gareth as he stopped on the other side of the curb. "I figured, if we're gonna do this, we should all come." He glanced up at the house on the hill. "Is that the house?"

"Wait! You don't understand." Sami kept her voice as low as possible. "It's a trap!"

Everyone stopped.

"How do you know?" asked Kierra, alarmed.

"Ask him." Sami pointed to Eddie.

Eddie looked as if someone had told a joke he didn't get. "Wha—?"

"Damon told me what Danner said." Sami felt her eyes burn as she addressed Eddie. "You didn't try out for the Safety Patrol. You're with *them*." She pointed to the house.

Eddie's eyes darted back, as if he'd been caught cheating on a test. "No! I mean, yes, it's true: I didn't try out for the Safety Patrol. But I don't work for *them*." There was contempt in his voice.

"Then why'd you lie?" Gareth said. His chest and arms puffed up as he approached Eddie.

"I was told to. The day before school began, a man and woman from the district came to my house. They said they wanted me to buddy up to Damon, to keep an eye on him, you know, 'cause they thought something like this might happen."

"So, all this Secret Club stuff," said Kierra. "You were just pretending?"

"No! I didn't know Damon was going to start a secret club—and I didn't tell the man and woman about it, either."

"Why not?"

"'Cause...the way Damon talked about wanting to save his friends...I wished somebody had been around to do that in the Forbidden Neighborhood. Maybe we could've helped Scotty and the other kids hurt by Old Lionel Perv."

Gareth turned away at the mention of his brother's name.

"And I guess," Eddie continued, "I wanted to be part of something bigger, something good...like the Power Club."

Sami didn't know whether to believe him or not. She turned to Kierra. "What do you think?"

Kierra shrugged.

"That's a big help!"

Sami looked up just in time to see a bird fly overhead, briefly illuminated by a street light. The bird was larger than the robins she normally saw in the district, and its colors seemed strange. But before she could remember where she'd seen them before, Gareth spoke.

"Listen, I've known Eddie most of my life. If he says he's not a traitor, I believe him." Gareth stared at the house. "Besides, if Old Lie is in there, I want him!"

Interlude 4

Just before hell broke loose, Lionel Viouet opened a window. Just before hell broke loose, Lionel Viouet spotted a bird. It was a most unusual bird—blue with green and gold feathers. He had not seen a bird like that in years.

A few minutes before hell broke loose, Lionel was listening, bored, to the argument. The Doc wanted them to move their base of operations, but the Calvin kid wanted to stay put—some emotional attachment to the house. The other kid, Rusty, got into an argument with Calvin, but it was clear that Cal had the upper hand. Teenage boys can be so touchy.

It didn't matter to Lionel where they went. He had done his part. Impersonating the Danner boy was easy enough. Lionel lured Damon Neumeyer out into the open so Calvin could drop the whammy on him. Now all of Calvin's enemies had been eliminated. What else was there to do but wait for more orders from the Liberator?

Lionel almost regretted the day he took the Liberator up on his offer. Lionel was on his own after having been forced to flee from the Forbidden Neighborhood; but he had his power, and that was enough. He could be anyone he wanted to be, anyone he needed to be. There was only one problem. He still had the addiction, the unholy desire that followed him wherever he went. He couldn't help himself, he told himself. The addiction always gave him away. Each time he gave into it, he had to flee and start over.

Then the Liberator found him.

The Liberator promised him haven and more—an end to his addiction. The Liberator's people were working on a cure. Lionel thought the Liberator was lying, but what choice did he have? It was better than facing life on his own, going from place to place and taking the risk of being captured. Lionel didn't give a damn about the Liberator's war or about ords. He just wanted the addiction to go away.

Calvin and Doc were arguing again. Cal reminded Doc that it was he, Cal, who had come up with this plan. Somehow, he persuaded the Liberator to launch this foolhardy mission: recruit powered kids in secret to start a war with ords. It all sounded so Third Reich to Lionel, but nevertheless that's what they were doing and where they were—cooped up in a house that hadn't seen air conditioning or a good dusting in months. Lionel couldn't stand it, so he opened a window.

The fluttering of the bird startled him and, as it flew away, he recognized it. The Forbidden Neighborhood was home to a lot of people with dangerous powers—shape shifters, mostly, and he remembered the girl Toni from down the street. What was she doing here? There could be only one explanation.

He turned to tell Calvin and the rest that someone was spying on them, and that's when hell broke loose.

Interlude 5

Sami said they needed a plan. She didn't mean for it to involve her climbing the stairs alone. Logically, it made sense. They needed more intel, Eddie said. He annoyed Sami when he tried to sound like a TV detective, but he was right. They needed to know what was going on in the house, and how many people were inside. The only way was for Sami to get closer.

Kierra suggested they hide until Sami returned.

"But what if I don't return?" Sami asked, terrified of the prospect of Calvin sending her away.

Eddie flashed a smile. "Don't worry! We'll come after you." He dove into one of the bushes. Gareth and Kierra crawled into another bush—together, Sami noticed.

She had been to Calvin's house before. They played together until the second grade, when Calvin sent Suzy away. The old side yard was familiar. It was where they played hopscotch and hide and seek. In the kitchen, Calvin's mom taught Sami how to braid her hair—something Sami's own mother never did. It was hard to think about it now, but this was almost her second home.

She paused by the window of the living room and listened. Voices. Arguing. Three distinct male voices. No, four. Calvin's voice she recognized. All that bad grammar and dropped *t*'s always annoyed her. There was another boy—one of the kids in the class ahead of Sami. Then the adult male voice she'd heard earlier. Up close, she recognized it from the demonstration on the first day of school. It was the counselor, Dr. Stone. *Figures. If Calvin wants to start a war, an adult would have to be involved.* There was a fourth voice she didn't recognize. *Must be your tree boy, Damon.*

She hoped to hear Damon's voice, too. Maybe he'd been captured and was inside the house. But no such luck. She listened a bit for other voices. Satisfied there were only four, she started to crawl back toward the stairs.

"I'm telling you, I know what I saw," the fourth voice said as it moved closer to the window. "We are being watched!"

Sami froze. Did they know about her?

A pair of footsteps moved closer. All that separated Sami from them was the wall of the house. She pressed her back against it as tightly as she could.

"It was jus' a bird!" Calvin jeered.

"A blue bird with green and gold feathers?" the other voice retorted. "They don't exist, Cal, except for this one girl who used to live in the Forbidden Neighborhood. Guess what. She's now a teacher at the school. I've seen her. And she was here, right on this windowsill."

They weren't talking about Sami. They must have been talking about Miss Vogel. She was here! Maybe she was still here somewhere. Maybe she had found Eddie and the others and was waiting for Sami to return. Maybe she had a better plan than barging into the house and fighting these guys. Sami resumed her crawl when her phone buzzed.

She fumbled to pull the phone out of her pocket and shut it off. The blue screen of an incoming call lit up the night like a torch. *Not now, Mr. Kytel!*

"Well, well! What have we here?" said the fourth voice as its owner leaned out the window.

Sami looked up as something black, like a manta ray, flew toward her.

Part II

Chapter One
Damon vs. The Power Club

"I think he's coming around."

"'Bout friggin' time!"

The first voice belonged to Ali. The second, though deeper than the last time he'd heard it, was Vee's. Was Damon dreaming?

Someone cupped a hand behind Damon's head and lifted him. "Damon?" It was Denise's voice. "Damon, you hit your head when you fell. Please wake up if you can."

It was no dream. As awareness returned, Damon felt heat through his clothes and all around his face and neck. *But it's August. It was cool a moment ago.* His hands felt hot, too, and he became aware that he was gripping something—coarse, granular. *Sand.*

No. Not again. Not again. If Damon wished it enough, maybe it wouldn't be true.

"Damon, we need you to wake up." It was Denise again, urgent, scared. *We.* Damn you, Calvin. Damn you to hell. Why'd you have to send them here? But maybe here wasn't here. Maybe it was some place entirely different. That's it. Damon had fallen and hit his head at Calvin's. They thought he was dead and just left him there. And then Denise and Vee and Ali came around and found him. That's what happened. Just like in the comic books.

He took a breath and choked on the thin, hot atmosphere. As he bent over to wretch, he opened his eyes and shut them again. The memory of the bright orange light lingered. He squeezed his eyes tight to make it go away. "Where am I?"

"I think you know," Denise answered. "I think you've been here before."

Something in her voice gave him the resolve to open his eyes again, to face reality. His vision blurred, and he became aware of a dull throb on the left side of his head, just above the temple. He rubbed his head as his vision cleared. Vague images of yellow and orange coalesced into a hill made of sand that stretched as far as he could see. As he looked up, he saw the sky—orange, just as it was before.

"Great! You're awake," said Vee as he bent over into view. Damon barely recognized him. He had grown his hair out but shaved the sides. The top was dyed neon blonde. He wore a black tee shirt covered with skulls. "Now you can contact your new team and make them get us out of here."

Damon tried to work his mouth, but his voice didn't come.

"Give him time," Ali said. Damon followed her voice and found her standing a few feet away, wearing a salmon top and red pants. Her brown hair wafted in the hot breeze, and she smiled at Damon with confidence. "Let him get his bearings, and then he can do whatever it is he does." It made Damon uncomfortable that she referred to him in third person.

Behind Ali, down the slope, he noticed two more figures. One was Danner. Damon wasn't surprised to see him, but sad nonetheless. He hoped at least Danner would have gotten away, but that must have been his real Safety Patrol jacket the shape changer was wearing. Danner bent down and spoke to someone. At first Damon thought it was Kyle, but this kid was too young. He had matted light hair and sweat-stained gray shirt and pants. He sat with his legs crossed and rocked back and forth.

"Who?" Damon managed to say.

"He says his name is Jayden," said Ali. "That's all we can get out of him."

"He was here before any of us." Denise said. She was kneeling next to Damon and helped him sit up. "Slowly," she said. Her hair was pulled back into a pony tail and her skin was red from being in the sun—or suns—too long. She wore new jeans and a green top with her shoulders exposed. "I was waiting on the bus to meet your new club when Calvin surprised me. He...he grabbed my purse before he opened a rift and sent me here."

Stealing a purse seemed strange, even for Calvin, but what seemed even more bizarre was that Denise had gone to so much effort to meet the Secret Club. "Why were you waiting on a bus?"

"Because we don't live across the alley anymore. Remember?"

Damon remembered. Denise and Vee and their parents had moved into a different house when they learned they would be expecting a new brother or sister. Denise told Damon this, but he had put it out of his mind. He never saw any moving vans, and he hadn't been asked to help with the move, like when Kyle moved. So far as he knew, they had never left. But they had left, and Denise and Vee had both changed. And Damon had missed out on it.

The heavy heat weighed him down as he stood. Sweat trickled down his arms and through his clothes. The thin atmosphere made it difficult to catch a full breath. He looked up for final confirmation of where they were. There were two suns, just like last year, though they seemed smaller than Damon remembered.

"So, when are you gonna get us out of here?" said Vee with impatience. He paced back and forth as if he were straining not to move too quickly. "Neesy told us about your secret club," he said, using the nickname he often used for his sister. "So, what're they gonna do? Force Calvin to open another rift?"

Damon shot a look at Denise, but she only stared at him without emotion—the expression she often used when she had seen something in her visions but was holding back.

"They're not coming," he blurted out. "Well, Sami came, but she's hiding in the bushes in front of Calvin's house." He told them about the others, how Gareth didn't answer, how Kierra wouldn't come, and how Eddie...Eddie was probably working with Calvin.

Vee and Ali and Danner—who had joined them—stared dumbfounded. Denise's eyes widened and then narrowed.

"No, it's not supposed to happen that way!" she said. "We fight Calvin in his house. I've seen it. They get us home."

"How?" Damon shifted the blame back to her. He didn't like the way the others were staring at him, as if it were all his fault.

"My visions are never wrong," she replied.

"No, but they are incomplete," Damon argued.

"So, we're not going home?" Ali asked, panic rising in her voice. "Ever?"

"We're stuck here?" Vee spoke fast, as he often did when he was agitated.

"You screwed it up!" said Danner, glaring at Damon.

"No, I didn't!" he shouted. "I did everything Denise told me to do. If she had given me more information...if her visions were more reliable—"

Sand showered Damon. It took him a second to realize that Vee had kicked a small mound of sand at super-speed.

"Don't yell at my sister!" Vee ordered.

Damon stood there, covered in sand, his exposed skin burning. He felt like a fool as the others yelled at him, telling him it was his fault or demanding he find some way to send them home. He breathed heavily, not knowing whether to cry or get angry. Finally, he chose to give in to the anger and let the dark space come.

"He's creating a dark space!" Denise shouted a second before he exhaled.

"No-he's-not!" Vee turned into a blur and rushed Damon. His super-speed push sent Damon flying backwards through the scorching air.

Damon didn't know how it happened, but through instinct he reached behind him and felt something leave his body like the dark space did when he exhaled. When he landed, he landed on something soft, something that wasn't there. Scared at first, he didn't want to look. But slowly he did. He was laying on a cushion made of darkness. *His* darkness.

The dark space was solid.

It didn't feel like a mattress or a board. It didn't feel like anything. It was just there. He pressed against it with his hand, and it pressed back—a solid *force*. Damon felt giddy.

Vee and the others stood there, their mouths agape.

"See? I told you his dark space can do things he didn't tell us!" Danner said. "Maybe he can send us home!"

"Send-us-home!" Vee turned into a blur and ran toward Damon.

Tired of the lies, tired of being blamed for everything, Damon reached forward. He didn't have to concentrate much. A bolt of darkness shot forth, its rounded edge resembling a Hulk-sized fist. There was no way for Vee to avoid it. He collided with the fist, which caused him to ricochet. At super-speed, he bounced back toward the others. Ali instinctively flew out of the way. Denise ducked. Danner grew to giant size and prepared to catch the speeding bullet. It collided with him and sent them both tumbling.

Damon stared at his hand. An aura of darkness wafted smoke-like from his fingers. He had never felt so powerful.

A buzz permeated the air. Vee, recovered, ran up the hill on Damon's left. In the thinner atmosphere, his movements were slower than normal and sluggish, giving Damon time to reach forward again and push. Another dark bolt came, but Vee was far enough away to dodge it. The Vee-blur leaped on top of Damon and pushed him to the ground, then pummeled him at super-speed—so fast, the blows didn't register, but Damon knew what was happening and he couldn't concentrate enough for another push.

Another instinct. His body went limp, and he no longer felt the blows. He opened his eyes to see darkness. Vee's fists appeared momentarily in the cloud, pounding nothing. It was as if Damon's body had turned into darkness. He gave another push to bump Vee off himself.

The pain of the blows finally registered. Damon doubled over, clutching his ribs and stomach. As the darkness vanished, he felt nauseous and spat up blood. Someone kicked him from behind. He looked up to see Ali hovering over him.

"Send us back!" she shouted.

Damon felt an anger he had never felt before. Ali, who had always been nice to him, had kicked him. He reached forward and pushed.

The dark bolt shoved her into the sky.

Vee resumed his rapid-fire assault. Before Damon knew it, he was face down in the burning sand and being pummeled again. *What's the use? They'll never believe me. Why don't I just give up?* He surrendered to a different kind of darkness, but then the blows ceased.

Choking on sand and blood, he rolled to his side. Standing over him was a twenty-foot-tall Danner, holding Vee in a bear lock. Vee's arms and legs resisted at super-speed, but to no avail.

"LET-ME-GO!" Vee shouted.

"Stop it!" Danner ordered. "Fighting won't get us home!"

Vee fell limp in Danner's arms, panting from used-up oxygen.

Damon didn't try to stop the tears. He didn't care how bad crying looked in front of the others. Danner—the guy who had always been Damon's enemy—had just saved his life.

Chapter Two
The Dark Disc

"Don't those suns ever set?" Danner squinted up at the sky.

No, they don't. Damon didn't feel like sharing what he knew. In all the time he'd been in the orange dimension—hours, it must have been—the two suns never moved. But something was different. The air wasn't as hot as he remembered. Even the sand had cooled. Damon could sit for several minutes without worrying about the sand, as uncomfortable as it was, burning through his pants. The others also sat, shifting positions or standing occasionally.

Denise sat with her arms folded, her hands covering her already red shoulders. She exposed a shoulder so she could accept the chunk of power bar Ali gave her. Ali broke off more chunks of the melting snack and passed it to the others, even Jayden, whom they'd coaxed into joining them. Everyone except Damon. He sat away from the others, not welcome in their circle.

"Maybe Calvin will bring us back," Ali opined. "Now that he's punished us by sending us here, there's no reason to keep us here."

"But why's he punishing us?" asked Danner, as he nibbled on the chocolate and nuts. "I mean, you and me didn't have anything to do with rescuing Damon. We weren't even there." He glanced around. "I can't believe this place really exists. I thought Damon made it up."

Damon hated being talked about in third person, as if he weren't there. His head still throbbed from where he'd landed, and now his ribs and stomach ached from Vee's blows. If he were home, his mother would comfort him, put him to bed, and bring him whatever he wanted to eat. Chicken soup sounded good right now. Anything sounded good. Even a chunk of chocolate and peanut power bar. Damon eyed the snack as the others ate it, longing, but he didn't dare ask.

His mother and Eldon would be worried about him by now. He wondered if they'd called the police, like Denise's and Vee's parents did. He hated that thought. His mother worried about him anyway. His disappearance would drive her crazy. *Especially after Dad.*

He buried his face in his sleeve, not wanting the others to see the tears.

They spoke about what they had already discovered. There were no caves and no shelter nearby, only sand. Endless sand.

"What do we do?" asked Vee, anxious.

"We wait it out," Danner declared. "Denise said we would be back at Calvin's, fighting him, so he must bring us back eventually."

Ali jumped up suddenly. "God, I can't stand those suns! I wish they would set or do something!"

The heat was getting to Damon, too, and he was tired. Time moved differently in his dimension, but his body was still on earth time. It must have been more than twenty-four hours since he woke up and went to school. It seemed so long ago.

He couldn't make the suns set, but he could do something— something he hadn't tried in a year. He exhaled slowly. A dark space emerged, tiny, cloudlike. He reached up with both hands and held it like a baby.

"What's he doing?" Ali whispered.

"Damon's going nuts!" Vee shouted. The others laughed.

Let them laugh. Damon moved his hands around the cloud of darkness, shaping it, smoothing it out—and expanding it. The cloud took on the shape of a disc. Damon flattened it even further and stretched it out as far as his arms could reach, then he carefully lifted it over his head. Under the shade of his dark disc, the temperature dropped.

"Oh great!" said Danner. "At least Damon can be cool."
Still in third person. O ye of little faith.

Denise rubbed her shoulders. "Damon, can we...can we join you under there?" It was a plea of desperation.

If he said no, Damon wondered what they would do. But saying no wasn't an option. It galled Damon to be nice to these kids who weren't nice to him, but it was the right thing to do. He concentrated. It was harder to make the disc bigger than his arms could reach, but slowly the disc expanded in every direction. Denise scooted towards Damon. The others followed her lead.

Damon felt like a cross-legged guru, with his arms outstretched and the others surrounding him like followers. They relaxed and *oohed* and *ahhed* in the shade. It was a silly image, but it made Damon feel better knowing he had something to contribute.

"Thanks, Damon," said Ali. "I'm sorry we were mad at you." She broke off a piece of power bar and offered it to him.

"I can't..." Damon said, indicating that he needed to keep his arms raised to maintain the dark disc.

"That's okay," she replied. "I'll feed you." She lifted the piece of candy to his mouth, and he bit it, his lips momentarily touching her fingers. Damon tried not to make a big deal of it, but she giggled and looked embarrassed.

The melted chocolate tasted like water, and the nuts and caramel made his mouth dry, but at least it was food.

~ * ~

Sand flew in two directions, leaving behind a trench as Vee ran at super-speed. He returned from the east—at least what they decided was east based on the position of the suns—and reported, "Nothing. It's just like Damon said. There are no trees or caves. Just sand."

Ali had flown into the sky earlier and looked up and down the slope to report the same thing. However, she couldn't stay in the air very long because of the suns.

At least everyone felt refreshed thanks to Damon's dark disc. He couldn't maintain it for long, but everyone panicked less and talked more, formulating a plan. Ali had two more power bars in her belt purse (Damon wondered why Calvin and his gang hadn't taken it like they took Denise's purse and Danner's jacket), so they wouldn't starve, but water would be a problem. So would sleep.

Denise had spent the time waiting for her brother to return with her eyes closed, trying to conjure up visions. "I've been practicing with a special coach at school," she said. "I can sometimes see things that will happen a few minutes or a few seconds in the future. That's how I knew you were going to create a dark space earlier." She opened her eyes. "Just like I know you're going to tell us about an oasis."

Damon searched his mind. He had no idea what she was talking about.

"An oasis?" Danner asked. "That's like a place in the desert where there's food and water, right?" He glared at Damon. "You know where it is?" It sounded more like a threat than a question.

Damon thought back to his earlier visit to the orange dimension. He hadn't seen anything with food or water, but he wasn't alone. Calvin had trapped an ex-friend of his named Larry there, too, and Larry said—

"Larry said there was an oasis at the bottom of the slope. But he had tried to climb back up the hill and was almost dead when I found him. I thought he was delusional."

"Down the slope?" Danner asked. "How far?"

Damon shrugged. "Like I said, I thought he made it up."

"Why was he trying to climb back up the hill?" Ali asked.

"He wanted to be where Calvin dropped him. He thought Calvin might let him come back home."

"So, we should stay here!" said Vee, excited. "In case Calvin opens another rift."

"But how long will that be?" asked Danner.

"Calvin won't open another rift."

The voice came from Jayden. Damon had almost forgot he was there. Jayden spoke in monotone, as if he were relating some distant story.

"Calvin wants to keep us here forever."

"How do you know?" Ali asked.

"Yeah," Danner said, "how do *you* know?"

The boy dropped his gaze. Damon took his first good look at him. He seemed to be ten or eleven, had close-cropped light hair, and his skin was brown—Damon assumed—from being in the suns so long. It wasn't a tee-shirt he was wearing but a plain grey shirt without a collar. His matching pants had no pockets. It looked like a uniform. Jayden tightened his mouth. He would say no more.

"Tell us!" Danner barked as he took a step toward the boy.

Not wanting to see the boy bullied triggered another memory in Damon. "Guys, Larry thought he'd only been here a few days. But time passes differently in this dimension. Do you remember how long he'd been missing?"

The others shrugged or shook their heads.

"A month."

The revelation had the desired effect. Danner backed away from Jayden. But it also sent shockwaves through everyone.

"A month?!" Vee said. "You mean we can be here a month?"

"Or longer?" Ali raised her voice.

"We won't be here forever!" Denise argued. "I've seen it. We'll be back in Calvin's house, fighting him."

"Yeah, just like Damon's new club is coming to rescue us?" Vee turned on his sister. "Neesy, sometimes your visions don't come true and you know it!"

Denise looked as if she had been punched in the gut. All eyes were on her.

"That's not true!" she spat at Vee. "THAT'S NOT TRUE!" She turned away from everyone.

No one said anything. Finally, Danner spoke.

"So, I guess we have only one choice."

"The oasis?" Damon asked.

"The oasis."

Chapter Three
The Journey Begins

They walked for what seemed to Damon to be an eighth of a mile. He had once walked the running track of the high school on a field trip and this is what that felt like. At first he felt invigorated to be walking downhill with a goal in mind. He could see it in the others as well: a cautious hope that they would find the oasis with food and water. But the sameness of the sand and orange sky made that hope too exhausting to maintain. Fear crept in, reminding Damon that Larry might have been delusional. Was this trip for nothing?

Jayden collapsed to his knees.

"Get up," Danner urged him. "We've got to keep moving."

Jayden stared at the ground, the dark circles under his eyes making him look like a raccoon. "Tired," he said in that monotone voice. Then he laid down, curled up into a ball, and closed his eyes.

"What's wrong with him?" Ali asked, worried.

Vee picked up the younger boy's arm and tried to pull him up to no avail. Jayden's breathing settled into a gentle rhythm, and they realized he had fallen asleep.

"That's what we all should be doing," said Denise. "How long have we been up?"

"I stayed up for twenty-four hours straight once," answered Vee. "That's what this feels like. Of course, with my super-fast metabolism, I build energy quickly." He moved back and forth in a blur to illustrate his point.

"And you burn it even quicker!" Denise retorted.

Vee looked deflated.

Ali shielded her eyes as she looked up at the suns. "Even if we could sleep, we can't do it here, underneath the suns. The sand would burn us, too."

"I may be able to help," Damon offered. His mouth was even drier from eating the chunk of power bar and the copious amounts of sweat that had left his body. He could only imagine a cool drink of water at the oasis, if it existed. "I can sometimes create a dark space and maintain it while I sleep." He recalled how he had awoken the other day, realizing his cloud of blackness had activated itself. "I could try it," he announced, uncertain.

No one argued. That in itself told Damon how tired everyone was. The notion that they would consent to his darkness when they still thought he could send them someplace else...well, Damon didn't want to dwell on it. He was just happy they were cooperating, that they had let him into their circle.

"What do you want us to do?" asked Ali.

"Just lay down like you normally do when you go to sleep. But it helps if we stay close together. I'm not sure how big of a dark space I can maintain."

The girls gravitated to one side of the hill and lay down. Vee and Danner chose spots close to Damon and Jayden. Damon sat, legs crossed, and tried to relax.

"Oh," Danner spoke softly, leaning up. "Just in case you're thinking about it, no funny business."

"What do you mean?"

Danner nodded toward the girls.

Damon knew what he meant and felt offended...that Danner thought he would take advantage of girls while they slept under his own darkness...that might be something Danner would do, but Damon would never think of it.

"I'm not like you!" Damon shot back.

"Oh, really?" Danner contorted his face into an odd grin and then scooted away from Damon. Vee, picking up on the cue, did likewise.

"I didn't mean like that," Damon said, embarrassed. "I meant..." But what did he mean? There was no way he could dig himself out of the hole Danner had helped him dig.

"Just get on with it," Danner ordered. He closed his eyes, signaling the end of the conversation.

Now it was even harder for Damon to relax. He took several deep breaths, letting the darkness build within him, cool him from within. Then he exhaled. The darkness covered him and spread across the others like a gentle blanket. In black and white, he observed the exhausted bodies around him. It was like they were only camping out at night or on a lunar landscape. Damon felt invigorated thinking of his favorite show, *Star Seekers*.

He reached forward with his finger and thumb and pretended to unzip something. The gesture was unnecessary, but it made him feel more like a Star Seeker.

"I've opened a sound space so we can hear each other," he announced. "Just call out if an alien sand crab bites you." The lame joke was met with groans—and snoring. The snoring came from Danner. Damon closed the sound space slightly in his direction, muting the snoring. He then laid back and stared at the black sky of his own creation. They would get out of this somehow.

~ * ~

"Damon, wake up."

"Just a few more minutes, Mom." Damon's mouth and throat were parched, but the sleep felt so good.

Snickering.

"I'm not your mom." A rude kick to the shin. "Your dark space vanished."

Damon woke to find Danner standing over him. The other boy's face looked dirty, and Damon realized Danner hadn't shaved.

"H-how long?" It hurt to speak.

"How should I know?" Danner walked away.

Damon reset his watch, hoping something had changed. When he had first arrived in this dimension, the black-faced digital—a birthday present from his mother—had gone haywire, the numbers flashing at random. Damon had shut it off and rebooted it. The numbers displayed

0:00. This time, the display read E:EE.

Damon looked away so the others couldn't see his disappointment. None of them had watches. They had phones. But their phones were all in their purses or jackets or otherwise back in their own dimension.

Ali screamed.

Damon pulled himself together as he ran to see what was wrong. He joined the others beside Ali, who knelt next to her belt purse, which she had taken off to sleep. In the sand next to it lay the wrappers of the two remaining power bars—empty except for smears of chocolate and the odd pecan. Something moved across the wrappers—something tiny and white.

"There are maggots on this world!" Vee exclaimed.

"Worse," said Danner, "the maggots just ate our food!"

Ali looked up at the others, an expression of hopelessness and hunger. "I'm sorry! I'm sorry!" she mumbled.

Damon wanted to tell her it wasn't her fault, but he lacked the energy to speak.

"Look!" said Jayden, who spoke so rarely Damon didn't recognize his voice at first. The young boy was standing away from the others and pointing to the sky. The two suns had parted and moved a noticeable distance away from each other. They were also smaller.

"What's happening?" asked Vee.

Damon remembered something he'd seen on TV. "We must be on a planet with an elliptical orbit." The others stared at him blankly. "Didn't you guys ever watch *Star Seekers*? They were trapped on this planet once which rotated around its sun on an elliptical orbit." He bent down and drew a diagram in the sand. "Look, this is how earth rotates around our sun." He drew a circle around another circle. "But this is a planet with an elliptical orbit." He drew a circle with an oval around it. "When the planet moves along its orbit, it gets further and further away from the sun."

"Come on, that's just a stupid TV show," said Danner.

"No, it's not," said Denise. "I studied this in my science classes. It's real."

Not for the first time did Damon feel validated when Denise backed him up. Everyone regarded her as the smartest, not just because of her vision power, but because she was a science nerd.

"But why are the two suns moving apart?" asked Vee, who seemed to be full of questions.

"They must be on an elliptical orbit with each other." Damon drew another diagram. "Maybe this sun is stationary, but this one moves around it." He drew a circle and then an oval, then another oval around the first oval. "So, this is where we are." He pointed to the second oval.

The others stared at the drawing, their mouths hung open, their shoulders slumped. Damon realized what he had done. He had made the second oval so large that it seemed to be moving a great distance away from the circle and the first oval. Everyone knew what that meant: It would get cold and dark. Very cold and very dark.

Damon tried to make them feel better by reciting something else he had learned from the show. "But it may take years and years to get there. Some planets take decades, even centuries, to circle their suns."

"It could be even worse than that," said Denise, her voice anxious. "We may be moving away from one sun and toward the other."

"So, what happens if we get too close?" Vee again.

"If a planet gets too close to a sun, the atmosphere burns away and the ground turns into molten rock. But if a planet passes between the suns, the gravitational forces could tear it apart."

Everyone stared agape. Denise seemed surprised, as if what she had said was only theory, not something that applied to the very planet on which they were standing.

"Oh, my God!" she said, cupping her mouth with her hand, as if she just now realized how real her theory was.

Chapter Four
The Scout

Damon lost track of the back and forth arguments. There was crying and panic and shouting and blame, most of it directed at him. He shut himself down. He had tried to convince them that on *Star Seekers*, there was always hope. There was always a way. But it was just a stupid TV show, they reminded him. In the real world, there was no hope.

They were just kids, they told him, not heroes. None of them asked to have powers. None of them asked to be here. All of their choices had been taken away from them.

Seeing things through their eyes made Damon feel depressed. He wanted to remind them that they weren't just kids. They each had a special talent, an ability that made them unique—an ability that had allowed them to survive this far. If they worked together...but the idea sounded childish, naïve in his own mind. The darkness therein was all he had left...a darkness that told him *just give in, just give up*.

Somehow, the shouting had worked its way into a plan. Danner, shouting above the rest, said, "If we find food and water, we can work on finding a way home." He reminded everyone that Denise had said they would fight Calvin, so there must be a way home.

It was Vee who came up with the next part of the plan. "My metabolism has kicked in," he said, moving around with energy to prove it. "I can scout ahead to see how far away the oasis is."

"No, we should stay together," Denise said, her tone weak and halting by comparison.

"But if there's food, I can bring it back." Vee's enthusiasm mounted.

Everyone thought it was a good idea.

Denise shook her head. "No! What if you get lost? What if you don't come back?"

"Come on," Vee replied, an edge in his voice. "I'm not a little kid anymore. I don't do that."

Denise folded her arms and glared at him.

"Hey, don't we have a say in this?" said Danner.

Denise cast him a glance, shooting him down. "Mom and dad put me in charge," she said to Vee. "If anything happens to you, they'll kill me."

"But, come on!" Vee argued. "You guys are so weak, you can barely move. Ali, can you still fly?"

Ali looked uncertain, as if she hadn't thought about it until just now.

"I can save us all!" Vee stomped his foot on the ground at super-speed, causing sand to splatter. "Besides, you're my sister, not my jailer. I don't have to listen to you."

And that settled that.

They agreed that Vee would only go a short distance—he would count to 300 to measure time and then turn back. Ten minutes would make a good trial run, everyone thought. Vee stepped forward, his feet almost bouncing on air.

"I'll keep going until I find the oasis. If I don't, it won't matter anyway." He turned into a blur and took off before anyone could argue.

Ali moved next to Denise. "Don't worry. I can still fly. I'll watch him until he's out of sight."

Denise crossed her arms and refused to look at anyone.

Ali rose in the air, though her movements were wobbly. She reached a height of a hundred feet and hovered. To Damon, she resembled a toy bobbing in water. A breeze blew through her hair and ruffled her salmon shirt. Damon couldn't look away.

"He's cresting a dune..." she called down, "and another." She watched for a few more seconds and then slowly descended.

"Thank you," Denise said in a low voice. As she looked up, Damon saw she had been crying.

~ * ~

There was nothing else to do but resume their own slow trek down the hill.

Damon walked close to Danner, the girls hung together, and Jayden brought up the rear. Damon looked behind from time to time to make sure the younger boy hadn't laid down or gone to sleep again.

"Why do you think Calvin sent him here?" Damon asked.

Danner seemed annoyed at the question. "I don't know. He's your enemy, not mine." His tone made it clear that he still blamed Damon for getting them into this mess.

Damon wanted to make amends, even though he knew it wasn't his fault, not entirely. He also wanted to make amends with Danner for saving his life. Mostly, he just wanted to talk. "So, everything's going well, with the Safety Patrol, I mean?"

Danner continued to look straight ahead. "Sure, if you call being betrayed by Rusty and our own advisor fine."

"I mean other than that," said Damon, back tracking. "I think it was a good idea to form a club in school."

"You're still not getting in."

"That's not what I mean."

"Look, this could be a long trip. If we talk, we'll just burn up energy." Danner walked ahead.

Damon wanted to dig a hole in the sand and crawl into it. Maybe if he created another dark space or dark disc, things would be better, but it was difficult to maintain the dark disc while walking. Inside the dark space, they couldn't see where they were going anyway. It was the only talent Damon had, the only thing he could contribute to their survival, and it wasn't enough.

He glanced back and shouted, "Jayden's gone!"

Everybody looked around. There was no place he could run off to that they wouldn't see. They ran back to study the tracks they'd left in the sand. Everybody left their own tracks, and Jayden's small foot holes were easy to spot. They consisted of one hole in front of the other, until they stopped.

"It's like the sand swallowed him whole," Ali said.

116

"No, it's like he took off into the air," Damon observed.

Everyone looked up into the sky, but there was nothing.

"Or," Denise said carefully, "like a dimensional rift opened."

Everyone looked at each other and then away. It was too good to be true. But if it was...

Denise looked down the hill. "Vee should be back by now."

"It's only been seven minutes," said Danner. "I've been counting."

There was a sound Damon hadn't heard on this planet before. He thought he imagined it. But there it was again. *BOOP*. A mechanical noise. Then another. *BIP*.

"Shh! Shh, everyone!" said Ali. They all heard it.

BIP. BE-BEE. BOOP.

"It sounds like a game," Danner said.

Ali unzipped her belt purse and pulled out a Game Charger. The green, rectangular device looked like the one Damon had back home. The buttons at the bottom blinked, and the screen flashed through several games. Ali stared at it like it was an alien disease. "But I didn't turn it on."

The screen flashed again, its pixilated icons moving together to form an image. A nose. A mouth. A pair of eyes which opened and closed.

Damon recognized the face before anyone else. "It's Jayden! He's in the machine!"

Chapter Five
The Kid in the Machine

The face *smiled* at Damon. It was a weird kind of smile, consisting—as the rest of the face did—of icons, little grey boxes that resembled Chinese writing. The icons moved, not in the jerky way that game icons often did, but in a natural way, like a real face.

"How did he get in there?" Danner shouted.

"He must have a power," Denise reasoned.

Danner looked at her. "I thought he was an ord."

So did Damon. Jayden hadn't shown a power before, so Damon assumed he was some random ordinary kid Calvin had come across and sent here. But now it was starting to make more sense. Jayden's grey shirt and pocket-less pants. It was a uniform.

Ali held the Game Charger at arm's length.

"Don't drop it!" Denise cautioned her. "You might hurt him."

The face reacted as if it *heard* her. The icon mouth opened and closed as if it were speaking, but the only sounds that emerged from the machine were more *BOOP*s and *BIP*s. A pixilated brow furrowed, and then the screen went blank.

"What happened?" Ali looked terrified.

"Check the batteries," Danner urged her.

A fiery glow surrounded the Game Charger. Ali dropped the device and jumped back. The glow intensified and expanded.

"It's going to explode!" Danner shouted. Everyone ran in different directions.

But there was no explosion. The glow flowed like a fountain above the device and gradually took the form of a human boy. When the glow subsided, Jayden stood over the device as if he'd never left.

"Don't be afraid," he called out. "That's just my power. I can enter electronic and digital devices and control them." It was the most Jayden had said since they'd found him. He no longer spoke in monotone. His voice was happy and full of energy.

"So, why didn't you use it before?" Damon asked with caution.

"'Cause I didn't know you guys had a device, except for your watch, Damon, but it's too small. But when Ali's belt purse was open, when the sand maggots ate the power bars, I saw it. I had to get inside it so I could recharge."

"Recharge?" Ali had flown to escape the glow and still hovered ten feet off the ground. "What are you, some kind of android?"

"No," Jayden said with a self-conscious laugh, "but when my power gets low, I get low. I need to be recharged, just like any device."

Ali landed. Slowly, everyone started to move towards Jayden.

Denise asked what they all were thinking, "So, who are you, Jayden, and where are you from?"

Jayden picked up the Game Charger and offered it to Ali. "I didn't hurt it."

Reluctantly, she took it.

"My name is Jayden Ross," the boy answered. "I live in the district, or at least I used to. About six months ago, I wanted to visit my grandparents, but they live in Florida. So, when my parents weren't watching, I picked up the phone at home, dialed my grandma's number and entered the line. I travelled for a long, long, time, but her phone went to voicemail, and I bounced. When I came out of the phone line, I was somewhere else—North Carolina, I think.

"I tried to go back home, but I don't know geography. I ended up in Seattle. That's where they found me."

"Who?" Danner asked.

"The Liberator," answered Damon, putting it all together. "You're from the Liberator's compound, aren't you?"

Jayden hesitated, then nodded.

"The Liberator?" Ali repeated with disgust. "The terrorist who blows up airplanes?"

"I didn't know who he was." There was fear in Jayden's voice.

"He's got this ranch out in the middle of nowhere and he has other people working with him—Barney, Celia, Clive, Longtrees—and there are about fifty kids, all with powers." The information spilled out of him as if he were being interrogated. "He feeds us stuff that slowly retards our powers and we have to stay there and listen to his lectures before we can take the antidote."

"What kind of lectures?" asked Denise.

"About how ords are evil, how the Powers—that's what he calls us, the Powers—are going to rise up and overthrow them and start a new society with us in charge."

The idea made Damon sick. It confirmed what he already knew about Calvin, but to hear it again from this kid, this stranger, made it all the more real. And there were fifty more, just like Calvin and Rusty and Old Lie. "So, the reason Calvin returned to the district," Damon said, "was to recruit more kids?"

Jayden looked up at Damon. "Yeah, and to get revenge. He hates you, Damon, but he's also afraid of you."

"Afraid of dweeb face?" Danner sneered. "What for?"

The answer floored Damon. "Because he has friends—you guys. You helped him get out of this orange dimension the first time. Damon didn't force you to do anything or make you afraid or threaten you. You just did it. It was because of you that Calvin got arrested and had to escape from the district."

Ali shook her head. "But like Danner said, we weren't even there. I wanted to be—" Danner cast her a dirty look. "—but there was no time for Denise to call us. It was just her and Vee."

"And Kyle," Damon added, wanting to make sure their former member wasn't forgotten just because he'd lost his power.

Jayden lowered his head. "I'm afraid that's my fault. As soon as I could, I escaped from the ranch. But Calvin came after me. He caught up with me just after I returned to the district and found a surveillance center, which was closed. I found a tape of you guys. You were all there, in the mall, fighting protesters. Calvin must have watched it after he sent me here."

Damon remembered the battle at the mall—they all did. It was the first time the Power Club had worked together as a team. The first time they had acted like heroes. Now it was responsible for them all being trapped here, where they may never see home again.

~ * ~

They resumed their journey until Vee's tracks also stopped. Not like Jayden's, which had merely ended, but like the sand itself had conspired to remove the super-fast kid from the planet. There was a line where the sand shifted, like a scar, creating an uneven border that stretched as far as the eye could see. Beyond that, no more tracks.

"Vee!" Denise called, her parched voice cracking. "VEE!"

Danner grew to his maximum size of just over thirty feet so he could see over crests in the distance. Ali flew straight up so she could see even further.

Damon did the only thing he could do. He scanned the horizon in every direction. It made no sense—there would be tracks any way Vee went—but he had to do something. It was his fault they were trapped here. It was his fault that Vee ran off. It was his fault—

"Do you feel that?" Jayden called out. He had become impossibly perky since his "rest" inside Ali's Game Charger.

Damon felt wobbly, but he blamed lack of food and water and now worry over Vee's fate. He shook his head.

"Do you feel THAT?"

By the time Jayden had finished the question, they all felt it. The ground shook.

"Oh, great! An earthquake on top of everything!" Danner howled. He struggled to remain upright at his height.

The ground in front of them, just beyond the scar, sunk in on itself. It created a deafening DZZZLDZZZLDZZZL sound like water emptying in a drain. Damon, Danner, and Jayden ran back as far as they could, but Denise did not move.

"Denise, get away from there!" Ali called from the sky.

But Denise stood at the edge of the widening hole and stared as if she were waiting for something.

"She's transfixed!" Danner shouted.

Damon knew what that meant. Denise must be in shock. He became angry, not at her, but at himself for getting them all into this fix. He didn't care if he lived or died, but he was determined he wasn't going to lose anyone else. He heard Danner and Jayden call after him as he ran toward Denise.

As he reached her, he struggled not to lose his balance. The chasm had spread to just in front of her feet, and the sand flowed down around them like a waterfall. No, not just around them, *underneath* as well. The sand was pushing them toward the chasm.

"Denise, come on!" he shouted, grabbing her by the arm. She did not react. Her eyes were glassy. "This is no time to have a vision," he shouted. *"Come on!"*

The DZZLDZZL sound gave way to a rumbling—something was inside the chasm and it was coming up. Damon and Denise lost their balance and fell backwards in the sand. Helpless, they stared as a giant structure emerged—sand flowing from its top like a curtain.

"Hey, Damon," called Vee from somewhere inside, "did Larry say the oasis was underground?"

Chapter Six
The Oasis

To Damon, the thing resembled a giant merry-go-round—if a merry-go-round didn't have horses but instead had red and purple foliage resting atop spindly poles that swept gracefully out of a blue-grey ground. The poles passed for trees, he guessed. They covered the place, providing plenty of shade. Some of the trees had fragile-looking, coconut-shaped objects growing out of them.

In the middle stood an object that didn't look natural at all. It resembled a triangle, bent over on one side, made of diamond at the edges but otherwise translucent. It was half the size of a person, and behind it, with his hands on the edges and his legs outstretched stood Vee.

Denise rushed into the merry-go-round and threw her arms around her brother.

Damon looked at Danner and Jayden, who hung back, cautious.

Ali landed next to Damon, her eyes darting all over the new place. "What is it?"

Like I know. Damon took a step forward. The blue-grey ground was soft, but it held. As he examined it closer he saw that the ground was made up of thick granules, different from the sand. His feet did not sink into these clusters. They pushed back firmly, like rubber. He took another step. Nothing happened. He bounced up and down on the ground. It held.

"Welcome to our humble home!" said Vee, coming around the triangular object to join them.

"But how did you find it?"

"That diamond triangle is a lever. When I came across it in the sand, I tried to figure out what it was and somehow activated it. It caused this place to appear. Then when I touched the lever again, it took me down inside."

"Down inside...the planet?" said Denise, wiping away tears of joy.

"You should see it! It's huge down there. Like a city, but made of this stuff." He pointed to the pole-like trees. "But, so far as I could tell, nobody's there."

"But somebody must have built it," Damon said, studying the lever and the arrangement of the trees into a nice, tight circle. There was no way this place could be natural to this world.

"I don't believe in aliens," said Danner, who had joined them.

I don't either. Damon didn't say it aloud in case somebody—or something—was listening.

"Is there food down there?" asked Jayden.

"He speaks!" said Vee, surprised. "Yes, there's food. It's this stuff." He pointed to the coconut-shaped objects growing out of the trees. He sprinted over to one and yanked it off the tree, which made a high-pitched keening sound, as if it were in pain. Vee brought the object over to the rest. It was light in color but covered with dark splotches that formed irregular patterns. It reminded Damon of a chocolate-covered Easter egg.

Denise looked at Vee, uncertain. "How do you know it's food?"

"'Cause I ate one."

"You idiot! What if it's poison?"

Vee looked hurt. "Look, if we don't eat it, we're all gonna die anyway, so we might as well..." His voice trailed off as he saw Denise's tight expression. Damon imagined what he thought she was thinking. *Irresponsible Vee. Always getting into trouble. Always acting before he thinks.* "Look, I ate it maybe fifteen, twenty minutes ago, and I feel great! I didn't grow a tail or anything."

"Well, you're right about one thing," said Danner, taking the object. "It's better than starving to death." He moved the object around in his hands. It *swished*, as if there were liquid inside. "How do we eat it?"

"Dig into it with your thumbs," Vee answered. Damon thought he saw Vee suppress a grin.

Danner plunged his thumbs into the object. It cracked open, and a crème-colored liquid splashed out followed by a smell—a smell Damon could only describe as broccoli covered with honey and toilet bowl cleaner.

It was the worst smell he had ever smelled.

Everybody agreed. Groans of disgust followed.

"Oh, I forgot to tell you," said Vee in full grin, "it tastes better than it smells."

If Vee pranked them, Damon concluded, it must be all right. He approached one of the trees and picked one of the objects. Its shell felt rough and sticky. Damon yanked it off the tree as he saw Vee do. The tree made the high-pitched keening sound.

"Sorry," Damon said, not sure to whom or what he was apologizing. He lifted the object to his mouth. The warm and creamy liquid poured down his throat.

~ * ~

Denise's scream woke them up.

She and Ali had decided to sleep in another part of the oasis, separate from the boys. Damon didn't know why, but he took it personally. After all, nothing had happened while they slept under his dark space. Even though they'd searched the oasis and didn't find anything that appeared to be dangerous, he thought they should stay together to be sure. But off the girls went while the guys lay down at what they decided was the entrance — the part facing the hill—and drifted off.

But now Denise was screaming. Everyone roused and ran to where the girls had made their haven. They found Ali leaning over Denise, trying to shake her awake.

"Let me do it!" said Vee, kneeling at his sister's side. "She gets this way sometimes when she has visions while she sleeps." He slipped his arm under Denise's back and guided her to a sitting position. Then he wrapped his arm around her head and gently rocked her. "The doctors said not to wake Denise while she's having a vision. It could kill her."

Ali jumped back. "I'm sorry. I didn't know."

"Shh!" Vee replied.

Denise's screams subsided into sobs, then she opened her eyes. They were glassy—an effect that always startled Damon. He thought he heard her mutter something. "Teeth."

The rocking continued for several seconds. Finally, Denise stirred and blinked. Her eyes returned to their normal piercing blue. She didn't act surprised that everyone was gathered around, staring at her.

"We're going to be attacked," she said in a distant voice. "Something with big, large, horrible teeth. Danner..." Her expression turned to sadness. "You're bleeding!"

Danner looked himself over. There was no blood. He had a funny look on his face, as if he half thought it was a joke.

"And Damon..."

Damon chilled as she gazed right through him.

"...you have to face Calvin alone."

There was a dread in her voice, a dread that made Damon wonder what would happen to the rest of them. She blinked again, then leaned into Vee's shoulder and cried.

The others stood in silence. They would get no more answers.

Danner tapped Damon on the chest and motioned to follow him. Jayden followed along. Back at the entrance, Danner turned to Damon.

"Maybe the district lied about you being able to make people disappear, but maybe not. You did some things with your darkness while you were fighting Vee, things I never saw you do before."

"I know," Damon replied, defensive. He didn't want to admit how little he knew about his dark space or what it could do. "But I don't know if I can do it again."

"Well, try!"

Damon looked around, not sure what to do. He could try to use a concussive force on one of the trees. *But what if it makes another keening sound? What if I hurt it?*

"I think I know the way home," Jayden said, "but it requires my power, not Damon's."

"What do you mean?" asked Danner.

"This isn't really another planet. It's another dimension. It's like a room in a house, like there's a curtain separating us from our own world."

"So?"

"So, just like I can travel through phone lines, I can also travel through digital devices. Maybe I can use one to travel through the curtain."

"You mean you can use the Game Charger to get us home? Why didn't you say so before?"

"No, not the Game Charger." Jayden laughed as if it were the stupidest idea ever. "It has to be a device that connects to other devices, like a phone."

Hope drained from Danner's face. "All our phones are back home. Mine's in my jacket pocket, and so's Ali's. Denise's is in her purse, and Vee keeps his on a belt clip which Calvin stole before he sent him here."

"Maybe that's why he took them," Jayden said. "Because he knew I could use them to get home. But what about Damon?"

"Dorkface doesn't even have a phone."

Damon started to say it wouldn't matter. If Jayden was correct, Calvin would have taken his phone, too. But something stirred in the back of his mind. All the times he wished his mother would let him have a phone...how he couldn't play games or surf the Internet or call friends or even call someone if he were in trouble...and then he remembered.

"I think I know where we can find one."

Chapter Seven
Up the Hill

Damon stared up the slope. It seemed unreal, impossible, and incredibly stupid that they would have to climb it. They'd only just found the oasis—a place of shade and food. It was a miracle it even existed. And there was the underground city to explore. And now they decided to leave it all to search for a phone—his phone.

Or rather, his mother's phone. The one she had loaned him when he went to Mack Park last year, just before Calvin sent him to the orange dimension.

So far as Damon knew, it was the only phone in this dimension and, thus, their only way home.

The red and purple foliage snapped as he pulled it out of the ground. They thought they could tie some if it—the ones that resembled leafy palm fronds—together to form something they could carry, but the fronds naturally stuck together. Some bending, some twisting, some shaping, and they had a red and purple sack large enough to carry five coconut-shaped objects, one for each person, for their journey.

They paused and took one last look at the oasis, the place which had been their home, their refuge, for the last several hours, or was it a day or two?

"I wish I had my phone to take pictures," Vee said. "They'll never believe this back home."

Damon wanted to burn the place in his memory so he could describe it later. He wasn't sure why. But they had gone places probably no one had ever gone before. They had seen evidence that there must be intelligent life somewhere outside of earth. And, so far, they had survived in a place that could easily kill them. It would make a hell of a story. If he could tell it.

He turned to Denise. "You said I have to face Calvin alone. That means I get home, right?"

Denise had been reluctant to say more about her vision. She waited a long time before speaking. "Either that, or he comes here. Or you both end up somewhere else. I can't be sure."

"Wait. Somewhere else?"

Denise turned away.

"We better get started," Danner announced to everyone. "Damon," he added with a threatening stare, "we'd better find that phone of yours."

"I can sense it," Jayden jumped in, "if we get close enough." He seemed impossibly happy and eager, a huge change from the kid who wouldn't speak when they first found him. "And we know we're going in the right direction, because the suns are in the same place in the sky that they were when Damon first came here, right?"

Damon looked up. The suns were in the same place—mostly. They had drifted further apart, and one sun had grown noticeably larger. It was a lousy way to navigate, but it was all they had.

"But will the phone still work after all this time?" asked Ali.

"It had a full charge when I left home," Damon replied, "and time passes differently in this dimension, so..." He shrugged.

"But what if the sand damaged it?"

Damon thought about that. He had kept the phone in the pocket of his old green windbreaker. When he lost the windbreaker, he lost the phone, but the phone would be protected—unless the sand maggots ate their way inside. But maybe sand maggots don't find phones as tasty as power bars. There were too many unknowns. He looked back at the oasis. Its weird foliage and bouncy ground looked inviting. Maybe they should just stay here—forever?

"I have to get home," said Denise, as if sensing what he was thinking. "My parents will be so worried about us."

They all nodded. They all had family, even Damon. He started to tear up.

"What's wrong?" Denise asked.

"I didn't say goodbye to Mom or Eldon when I left the house. Mom must have gone upstairs to the bathroom, so I just grabbed the key to the garage and left. I snuck out, like a thief." Confession was good for the soul Damon had heard, but saying this didn't make him feel better.

"It's okay, Damon," said Denise. "You'll see your family again."

"You're just saying that. Or are you having a vision?"

Denise smiled at him through the clearest eyes he had ever seen. "Neither. I just know you will."

~ * ~

Damon turned back from time to time until the oasis disappeared from view. He longed to go back and feel the shade again. He also wanted to explore the underground city, the city only Vee saw. The way forward was difficult. The way back was easy, inviting. If he looked forward, he saw only more sand and those suns. He felt out of breath just looking up the hill, at how far they had to climb, at the uncertainty that they would ever find his phone.

It was his turn to carry the sack with the food objects. Its weight seemed even greater.

About midday (he guessed it was midday), after they crested a third dune, they decided to rest and break into the food objects.

Damon pulled one out of the sack and dropped it.

It had changed.

The dark splotches that reminded him of chocolate had grown, taking over almost the entire shell. The shell had grown coarse and stickier, as if it were covered with mold.

Everyone stared at it.

"Are the rest that way?" Ali asked.

Not willing to touch another, Damon turned the sack upside down and shook it until the remaining four objects tumbled out. They had changed just like the first.

Danner swallowed, trying to suppress a look of disgust. "So what? Maybe the suns or the heat does something to them. Maybe they can still be eaten."

Vee looked askance. "You try it."

130

Danner picked up one of the objects. He moved it around in his hands, as if nothing was wrong with it. Finally, he cracked the shell with his thumbs.

No liquid spilled out this time.

"Ow!" Danner retracted his thumb and shook his hand. "Something bit me!"

He dropped the object, which broke in two, revealing a creature about the length of a ruler—pale white, with ridges along its armless and legless body. One end of the creature opened into a hole with tiny, sharp triangles covering the outside. Teeth.

Everyone jumped back.

The creature reared its mouth and twisted around, as if studying its surroundings and the people in it. Then it bent over, pushed its way into the sand, and disappeared.

"These things," Ali said, staring with horror at the other objects with horror, "they're eggs!"

Chapter Eight
Damon Helps Denise Get Her Bearings

They left the rest of the food objects behind and resumed their journey up the hill. But now they had nothing to eat.

The suns remained in the same position, but it was getting hotter.

"We'll never find the phone this way," Ali complained.

Danner, who walked in front, cast a glance at Damon. "How much further?"

Damon shielded his eyes as he looked up, trying to remember his position relative to the suns when he had lost the jacket. But that was a year ago.

"Maybe it's just over the next dune." An involuntary shrug told the others the truth; he really didn't know.

"Terrific!" Danner spat.

"I told you, I can sense it if we get close enough," said Jayden, imploring them to continue the trek for the phone.

"But how close do we have to be before you can sense it?" asked Danner with a skeptic tone.

"About a hundred feet."

That answer gave them some courage. They resumed the arduous task of putting one foot in front of the other.

Vee glared at the others impatiently. "We'll never make it this way. If I could find it myself, I'd run ahead again."

"Take Jayden with you," Ali suggested.

Everyone paused. It just might work.

"Come on, I can't carry a kid that big." Vee looked askance at Jayden. Even though the other boy was about three years younger, Vee was short for his age. He stood only half a head taller.

"Maybe he can ride inside the Game Charger," Danner suggested.

"I can't detect things when I'm already inside a machine," said Jayden, his energy and optimism waning. "It's like being inside a pinball machine and having balls going everywhere. There are too many distractions."

"Then," Damon said, "you'll have to ride piggy back."

Denise shot him a glance. "Didn't you just hear Vee? He said he can't carry a kid that big."

Somehow, hearing it from his sister provoked a change in Vee. He arched his back, as if preparing for an attack. "Well, maybe I can." He pretended to size up Jayden again. He bent down. "Hey, Jayden. Jump on my back."

Jayden obliged.

"Oof!" Vee buckled under the weight. "You're heavy for a ten-year-old."

"Eleven," Jayden shot back.

"Really?"

"Okay. Ten and three quarters."

Vee wrapped his hands under Jayden's knees for support and bounced up and down like a driver revving an engine. An unspoken decision had been made.

Danner, who still tried to sound like he was in charge, said, "Just go up a hundred feet and then come back."

"And then what?" Vee looked up at him with narrow eyes. His dyed blond hair was already soaked with sweat. "We'll just have to take off again. We'll keep going until we find Damon's phone."

Damon felt a pang in the pit of his stomach. It was his fault that they were there in the first place. Now it was because of him that Vee and Jayden had chosen to make a dangerous climb by themselves. If they never returned...

He was about to tell Vee not to go, that there must be a better way, but Vee turned to Jayden.

"Ready?"

"Ready."

A final revving, then the two boys blurred and shot up the hill, their form zigzagging as Vee struggled to balance the weight.

~ * ~

Ali walked ahead, next to Danner. They talked and flirted. Damon had always thought there was something between them, but he couldn't take his eyes off Ali. He remembered what Eddie said, that she was the girl of his dreams. Damon had thought it was a dumb thing to say. Not that she wasn't pretty, but she and Denise were part of the Power Club. They were teammates...even sisters to him.

But here they were, in this other dimension, and they might never make it home. Eddie's comment lingered, as did Danner's. *Don't try any funny business.* Damon knew what he meant, and he wouldn't have even thought of it if Danner hadn't said it. But Ali and Denise were becoming young women and Damon, though a year behind them was becoming a man. He hated thinking such thoughts, but he couldn't stop thinking them.

"Hey, Damon," said Denise, who had been walking some distance apart but now moved closer to Damon.

"Hey, Denise," he said and looked away, embarrassed. Did she see him looking at Ali?

"I told you my teachers are helping me control my visions. Well, I want to practice, and I need your help."

"What do you mean?"

She pointed to Damon's right. He looked over and saw an area of the hill which appeared more rugged, uneven. The sand clumped together in patches and rose in mini-dunes.

"I want to try walking up that area inside your dark space."

"But you won't be able to see."

"That's the point. If I can predict where to walk, then my power will grow stronger and I might even be able to see more of what I saw earlier—about Calvin, the monster and you fighting Calvin."

It was a tantalizing offer. If Denise could see more of her vision, she could see if they would all make it home. "Okay," he said, grateful for the distraction from his other thoughts.

They ran over to the rough area. Denise called to Ali and Danner and told them what they were doing, but Ali and Danner barely responded. They were too caught up in each other.

Up close, the rough area looked even rougher. Damon recalled the fissure he had seen in the sand, before the oasis appeared. The rough area looked like that, as if there had once been a hole in the sand, or several holes overlapping. Damon couldn't pretend to understand the physics involved, but it looked as if something had been there.

"I don't know about this," he said, treading carefully.

Denise acted as if she hadn't heard him. Possessed with her own project, she moved several feet away from him and closed her eyes. "I'm going to try to forget what this place looks like." She let out a huff of breath as if expelling unwanted memories. "Okay. Whenever you're ready."

Damon exhaled. The dark space surrounded the two of them. As his night vision kicked in, the terrain looked even more alien. The sand glowed white against the darkness, but it resembled carnage left from a bomb in a movie he had seen on TV.

In black and white, Denise resembled an old-time movie star. Damon caught himself staring at her, looked away, and then looked back. In the darkness she couldn't see him.

Denise opened her eyes and looked around, blind. "Damon? Damon, can you hear me?"

He opened a sound space. "Yeah."

"I've never been inside your dark space alone before." There was fear in her voice.

"You're not alone, I'm here." It sounded creepier than he intended.

"I know you're here and I'm glad. As long as you're here, I know I'm safe."

A warm feeling made Damon smile. Then he felt ashamed for staring at her.

"Okay," she said, shifting into project mode. "I'm going to force a vision. Whatever happens, don't help me. Don't tell me where to step. If I fall, don't help me up. Understand?"

"Understand. I mean, understood." Misspeaking was an attempt to make a joke, both to make Denise feel more comfortable and to cover his own mixed feelings, but the joke was lost on Denise. She bent over, as if studying something on the ground. When she looked back up, her eyes were glassy.

Throwing her shoulders back, she took a step. Then another. In front of her lay a depression in the sand. She paused, then stepped around it.

"Way to go, Denise!" Damon shouted.

"Shh!"

"Oh, sorry."

She took another step. Then another. Before her lay a mini-dune. She misjudged her footing and fell. She pushed herself up and paused. Then took another step.

It was excruciating watching her do this, but Damon had no choice. He couldn't help her. She had to do this on her own.

Another step, another fall. A ravine missed. Then another. She was making progress.

They reached the end of the rough area. The sand above it smoothed out, just like the rest. Damon held his breath as she paused. Would she predict this change? He waited for her to step out of the rough patch, to step confidently into the smooth sand, to turn to him and announce she had done it. He wanted to celebrate with her.

She turned in his direction, her eyes looked like mirrors that reflected nothing. "Damon! Cancel your dark space. Danner and Ali—they're in trouble!"

Chapter Nine
Worm

They couldn't really be called arms. There were too many of them. They looked like fringes sticking out of both sides of the large, flat body. The fringes moved back and forth in a distinct pattern, as if guided by some primitive intelligence. There was no separation between the head and the body, just a round bulb atop the fringes with a man-sized opening that must have been a mouth. It opened and closed at will, revealing triangular teeth. There were no eyes or nose to speak off—only dark splotches like those on the food objects back at the oasis. Damon could think of only one word to describe the creature. *Worm. A giant worm.*

It loomed before Ali and Danner, easily three times their size. They did not move. Damon and Denise stood half a yard below them. They, too, did not make any sudden movements.

The creature didn't either. It seemed to be studying them.

Danner turned his head slightly to Ali and said something Damon couldn't hear. In tandem, they backed away from the creature. The giant mouth lunged toward them, then reared back. They stopped.

Damon turned to Denise. "What do we do?" He hoped her vision, the one she had had inside the dark space, told her what to do next. But she stood there with a sick expression on her face.

"There's nothing we can do."

Damon refused to accept that. Earlier, he had used his dark space to create a concussive force, a physical presence that could push enemies away. He had a powerful *weapon* to use if he needed it. He inched closer.

"It won't work," Denise said.

Damon stared at her. She *had* seen something.

"What does it want?" Ali called out.

"Maybe it's come for its eggs," Danner replied.

They pointed down the hill, where they had left the remaining food objects. Damon and Denise joined them in pointing and shouting, "Down there! Down there! Your eggs are down there!"

The creature, if it heard or understood them, did not budge.

"It doesn't want us to move backwards," Danner told Ali, "but maybe we can move sideways."

Ali nodded and followed Danner as he inched to the creature's left.

The creature moved faster than Damon could blink. It leapt out of the hole in the ground it occupied and landed on a space between Ali and Danner and Damon and Denise. It reared back up to its full size, its mouth turning back and forth to both sets of teens. A high-pitched *screech* came from somewhere down inside the mouth. It chilled Damon's bones before it stopped.

Two things became instantly clear to Damon. The creature was intelligent, and it didn't want them to leave.

Danner sized it up. "Maybe I can scare it away."

Ali grabbed his shirt sleeve. "Are you crazy? Don't!"

"It's only about twenty feet long," Danner replied. "I can grow larger than that." As if to prove his point, he shot up to a head taller than the creature. "I don't want to scare it too much. I don't want it to attac—" The creature lunged, striking Danner in the chest.

Ali let out a startled gasp.

As Danner fell, the creature leaped on top of him. Danner kneed the creature. It jumped off. Danner scuffled to his feet, breathing heavily. "You wanna play it that way, huh?" He grew to his maximum height of just over 30 feet.

The creature, now dwarfed by its opponent, made a slithering motion in the sand. It seemed to be stalling for time.

"Got you scared now, don't I?" Danner taunted. He flexed his arms and started toward the creature, stomping his foot in the sand as if to send a barking dog scurrying.

But the creature didn't scurry. It stretched its body until it matched Danner's size.

Danner had a look of *Oh, crapt!* but he was already committed.

The thing lunged again. Danner held his ground as it met him head to head and they became locked in an embrace.

"I've got to try!" Damon shouted to Denise.

She said nothing as he ran to the giant combatants.

Damon stopped far enough away that he was out of reach of the thrashing tail. He pointed toward the creature and exhaled.

Nothing happened.

He pointed again. *Come on! Don't conk out on me now.*

Stubborn, the dark space refused to come.

The creature maneuvered itself closer to Danner. Its fringe-like limbs rose from its side and hardened, the edges sharpening, and dug into Danner's side. He screamed as he tried to push the creature back.

"Danner!" Ali called from somewhere behind Damon. "Just like we practiced at school."

She flew past Damon and circled the combatants like a large insect.

"No!" Danner cried through the pain. "Get back!"

She ignored him. Circling behind him, she shouted to the creature, "Hey, ugly! Try me!"

On command, Danner pushed the creature back far enough that its mouth chomped at the sky. Then Ali darted between Danner and the creature. The mouth turned to follow her movements, widening. Triangular teeth bore down on the flying girl.

Before it could bite, Danner planted a fist just below the mouth. The creature released its grip on Danner as it jumped back. Ali flew to safety.

The creature swooshed its tail in the sand and prepared for another lunge. Blood oozed down Danner's sides. They knew the maneuver wouldn't work again.

"Damon!" Denise called. "Get ready to hit the creature with your dark space!"

He shot a glance back at her. "But it doesn't work!"

"Just do it!"

Damon nodded, uncertain.

"Danner!" she called. "Shrink!"

Danner grimaced at the pain. "I can't—"

"Now!" Denise yelled.

He shrunk just as the creature lunged. It overshot him.

"Now, Damon!"

Damon pointed to the creature as it landed in the sand. He exhaled just as it turned around to face Danner again. A bolt of darkness shot from Damon's hand and struck the creature on the side of the mouth. It flinched, changed directions, and looked around, confused.

Emboldened, Damon pointed and exhaled again.

"No, don't!" Denise shouted, but it was too late. The dark bolt struck the creature on its side. But this time, it barely flinched. The head turned back and forth, its splotches forming a pattern that moved closer together. Finally, the head stopped as it zeroed in on Damon's location.

Oh, great! Now it knows where I am.

It hadn't occurred to Damon, until just then, that the creature—so used to darkness—might be blind in the sun. It reacted to movements, to attacks. And Damon had just given it a clue where to find him.

Danner, Ali, and even Denise shouted for him to get away, but they hadn't figured out what he just did. The creature would follow his movements.

He stood as still as he could and pointed. It was his only weapon. His only chance.

Something blurry struck the creature from behind, sending it toppling and tumbling in the sand.

"DAMON, GET OUT OF THE WAY!"

Vee!

Damon retreated down the hill as the blur ran around the creature, kicking sand at it. The creature bit at the blur but was always too late. It emitted another high-pitched screech. Then it reared up, dove into the sand, and disappeared.

Vee dropped to his knees, drenched in sweat, and panted. "We...won!"

"It might come back!" Damon called. He looked around and waited. They all did. "It senses movements," he shouted. "If we hold still..." They held still. A minute passed. Then another. The creature did not return. They had won, after all—for now.

"Over here!" Ali called. "Danner's hurt."

Danner lay in the sand with his head propped up on Ali's lap. The sides of his shirt and pants were smeared with blood. "I'm okay," he called. As if to prove it, he sat up and pulled up his shirt. There were scars where the creature had clawed into him.

"Your wounds have healed!" said Damon, incredulous.

"It's the way my power works," Danner said, smiling with relief. "I create extra mass when I grow, but the mass goes away when I shrink back to normal." His expression turned somber. "But if I grow again, the wounds will re-open."

"Then we've got to get you to a doctor," Ali said.

"Where's Jayden?" Damon asked.

Vee pointed up the hill. Jayden was jogging toward them, carrying something. When he got close enough, he held it up. Damon recognized the palm-sized object instantly.

"Hey, Damon!" Jayden called. "Here's your phone."

Chapter Ten
Damon Phones Home

The old flip-top looked tiny and cheap. It was hard to believe that it was their only chance of getting home.

"Does it still work?" Damon asked.

Jayden shrugged. "We were afraid to try." He offered Damon the phone.

"We had to dig for it," said Vee, still panting. "It was covered by several layers of sand, but it was still inside your jacket, Damon." He sounded proud, as if he had unearthed a buried treasure.

The others gathered around as Damon accepted the phone. He carefully raised the top. The blue LEDs behind the buttons lit up.

"It works! It works!" Ali squealed.

"What should I do?" Damon asked.

"Hold the phone in front of you and put it on speaker. Then call someone," Jayden answered. "But it's got to be someone who actually picks up the phone. If it goes to voicemail, I may bounce—like I did when I tried to call my grandparents."

Damon's mother was the obvious choice. She would probably recognize her old phone number on her new phone.

"What happens if you bounce?" Denise interrupted. "Where will you end up?"

"And how will you get *us* back?" Vee added.

"If I bounce," Jayden started, looking around, "I don't know where I will go. There aren't any phone lines or communications satellites here. Maybe I'll just cease to exist."

Everyone stared at him. Damon didn't know which bothered him more—the idea that Jayden might die or the matter-of-fact way in which he said it.

"As for the other question," Jayden continued, "somebody's got to make Calvin open another rift."

"Then we've got to call the district police," Danner insisted. "They can go arrest Calvin and then—"

"Then what?" Damon remembered that the police had kept Calvin's home under surveillance but were unable to catch him. If Calvin and the others saw the police coming and disappeared into another rift, they would never catch him. Calling his mother or any of their parents was also out since the police would now be monitoring their calls.

There was only one answer. Denise's vision—her original vision. Her visions since then had been stunningly accurate. She had predicted their every move during the battle with the worm. Maybe her original vision was correct, after all. It all rested with the Secret Club.

Damon pulled the scrap of paper out of his pocket and dialed the number of the one person who had answered every time he had called, the one person he could trust. He dialed Sami's number.

The search icon circled and circled. Damon remembered what had displayed last year when he tried to use the phone. He prayed it wouldn't happen again, but it did.

No network found.

"Don't worry about that," Jayden said. "Ever since Calvin started working with the Liberator, they were looking for ways to communicate between dimensions. There are now hidden networks. Give it a sec—"

"Hello?" came a voice from the other end of the phone. It wasn't Sami's voice. It belonged to a teenage boy—someone familiar—but before Damon recognized it, Jayden grew pixilated, like a computer version of himself. Then, in a flash of light, he entered the phone.

"Hey, Damon," said Danner, with an odd look on his face. "Who'd you call?"

"Sami Andrus." Damon started to explain that she was a member of the Secret Club and that they were the only people he could think of who could make Calvin open another rift, but Danner interrupted.

"So, how come Rusty answered the phone?"

It *was* Rusty's voice. Rusty—a member of the Safety Patrol. Rusty,

Calvin's friend.

"Hel—" the voice started again, then it cried out. Sounds of confusion followed. Damon heard Calvin say "Wha's he doing here?" Then Rusty: "Send him back! Send him back!"

The sky darkened. An area about fifteen feet above shimmered into a broad oval and opened. On the other side, Damon could clearly make out walls and a ceiling, as if he were looking up at them from a floor. Movement. And a flash of light. It was inside a house. *Calvin's* house.

"He did it!" Vee shouted. "He made Calvin open a rift!"

"But we'll never be able to reach it!" Denise lamented. She turned to Ali. "You're the only one who can make it. Go!"

Ali stared at the rift, uncertain. "But I can't leave you guys!"

"You won't have to!" Danner said. He concentrated and started to grow. The wounds on his sides split open. Blood spurted in every direction. At first, Danner didn't appear to notice. The wounds, Damon thought, must not be too bad. But, as Danner grew tall enough to reach the rift, the wounds became larger. He cried out.

He thrust his hands into the rift and grabbed the edges. The rift started to contract. Danner gripped it tighter. "He's trying to close it!" he shouted. He struggled to force the rift to remain open and widen it, and then, in one swift move, he forced the rift on its side and moved it toward the ground. An opening in the curtain, just ready for them to walk through.

"Hurry!" Danner shouted, his voice high pitched from pain.

Vee motioned for Denise to ride piggy back on him. She obliged. The two of them blurred and disappeared into the rift.

Ali flew into the rift next.

Damon wished he had some power to make a dramatic exit from the orange dimension, but running at normal speed would have to suffice. He could feel the cool night air, already. But, as he approached Danner, he saw just how much pain he was in. Blood oozed from Danner's sides. He breathed heavily as tears leaked from his eyes.

"How are you going to get back?" Damon asked.

Between breaths, Danner answered. "Just go!"

No. They'd come all this way together. They'd done so many things. Damon wasn't going to lose another friend. Damon stepped into the rift and exhaled. His power was darkness, but it was darkness that could be solid. He could create a concussive force with it. What else could he do?

The dark space always seemed to resist when Damon tried to do something new with it. It failed him when he needed it. Damon always thought of the dark space as his friend, as a part of him. But Damon decided that it was more, and he was more. He was the *master*, and it would do what he *wanted* it to do.

He manipulated the darkness as it appeared, flattening it and expanding it into a wedge.

Danner, realizing what Damon was doing, shifted his head and knee inside the rift.

Something yanked Damon inside the rift and pushed him face-first into the hard wood floor. He tried to rise. Something held him fast. He was surrounded by a force that appeared to be made of interlocking bricks. He had seen this effect before. At school.

Chapter Eleven
Into the Fire

He tried to push himself up, but the force field held firm. It was like his dark space—organic like the inside of a living thing—yet so different. It resembled crystal stones, reflecting light from somewhere outside and magnifying it. Damon could see he was on a hardwood floor, the same hardwood floor he had spied in Calvin's house. He lay prone, and the force appeared to cover him from head to toe. He heard running and shouting around him.

Through the opaque panes, he saw the room was dark, lit by a weak artificial light from somewhere. He recognized the picture window, boarded up from outside. Next to the it stood Vee and Denise, pressed against the wall. They were also encased in an opaque cage.

"Do something quick!" an adult male voice shouted. "I can't maintain the force fields for long."

Damon strained to shift so he could follow the sound of voice. Midway between his location and Vee and Denise's, he spotted a pair of brown dress shoes. He followed the leg up to an out-of-shape torso, clad in black, and a middle-aged face with curly grey-black hair. It was Doc Stone, the Special Club's advisor. He gestured toward Damon with one hand and toward Vee and Denise with the other. Wispy rays emanated from both hands, spread and crystallized into the cages.

So, that's how he did it. He has a power, too. Damon had thought the crystalline blocks that appeared momentarily at the demonstration were something artificial, just as the dragon was. But this teacher/advisor/district rep, whatever he was, he was one of them—and he worked for the Liberator.

"Just create another rift," Doc Stone barked, sweat visible on his brow. "Send them somewhere else!"

"I can' open another," Calvin answered from somewhere nearby.
"Not while one rift's still open!"

Good. Danner was still trying to get inside.

"Let us go!" Damon pleaded. "You're a teacher! How can you work
with them?"

Doc Stone peered down at Damon and smiled as if he were
addressing an unruly child. "I'm not a teacher—Damon, is it? I'm a
warrior. In every war, there must be casualties. You and your friends are
just that, casualties."

The crystalline cage tightened and pushed Damon against the floor.
From somewhere above him, he heard Ali cry out. He looked around, trying
to find her. In the far corner, he spied another girl sitting with her hands
and feet tied by a cord. Sami. *They got her, too.* Damon's heart sank.

Nearby, Calvin yelled, "Why'd you even answer the phone?"

Rusty bellowed, "'Cause it came from the secret number, the one
you guys created so you could call from other dimensions. I thought it was
you-know-who." He sounded excited, as if he had never spoken to *you-know-who.*

"Stupid!" Calvin hissed. "We coul' lose it all *tonight*, because of
you!"

Something in the way Calvin said "tonight" made Damon realize it
was still the same night—the day Calvin had sent them all away. In the
orange dimension he thought two or three days had passed, but time passed
differently there. In the back of his mind, he realized his mother and brother
didn't have much time to worry about him, if they even noticed he was
gone. Damon resolved that he would never give them anything to worry
about, ever again.

Ali screamed again. Her voice came from straight up. Damon
twisted his neck and saw her feet dangling from the ceiling. Above her,
attached to the ceiling, hung something black that resembled the manta ray
Damon had seen in the boys' room at school, the manta ray that could
change its shape.

"Stop struggling!" a voice called from the manta ray. It sounded
calm and amused. "Don't you know you can't get away from Old Lie?" It

was the same voice that belonged to "Tree boy."

Damon exhaled. The dark space spread through the crystalline cage and covered him completely.

"What do you think you're doing?" Doc Stone taunted him. "I've researched you, Damon. There's nothing your power of darkness can do inside my force field."

"Damon's hiding!" Rusty jeered from somewhere nearby. "You were right, Calvin! Without his friends, he's helpless!"

The word "helpless" rankled Damon, but the use of the word "friends" bothered him even more. It was true that Damon needed his friends. It was true that, without them, he had lost all interest in being a hero. It was true that he had tried to stand alone without them and failed. But that was all right. Calvin had made a big mistake in attacking his friends, and an even bigger mistake in sending them all away together. They had worked together to find a way back home. They were a team. An *unbeatable* team.

Damon concentrated. The dark space didn't resist this time. It hardened and grew stronger—a solid muscle and more. It pressed against the force field.

"What are you doing?" Doc Stone shouted. "Stop!"

The dark force pushed again. The force field buckled.

"Stop, I said!"

The force field tightened and pressed Damon into the floor. He could barely breathe. *I don't need to breathe. I AM the darkness.* He exhaled through every pore of his body and felt the dark force expand...outward, outward, ever larger, into eternity. At some point, the force field gave way.

Damon stood, his dark space covering the entire room. In black and white, he could see Doc Stone falter and fall against a wall. There was Calvin, his hair grown longer and wearing a grey suit similar to Jayden's. He stood in front of the rift, his attention focused on closing it, as Danner struggled to squeeze his shoulders into the tightening hole. Danner cried out, his face contorted by fear. He appeared to be weakening.

All Damon would have to do is walk up to Calvin and strike him. Then Danner could come home.

A burst of light appeared to Damon's right, like a lightbulb that had been turned on. The brightness and heat shook Damon and made him more aware of his physical body. Inside the light stood a figure with scraggly hair. "We gonna do this again, Neumeyer? I beat you in the alley last year. I can do it again."

Damon had forgotten about Rusty and his power to draw energy from the sun. But it was night. There was no sun.

"My power's grown," Rusty crowed. "I can store up energy for hours, even days. Now, get rid of the darkness or I'll hurt you!" It was a weak threat, the kind of threat they might have made in grade school, but Damon couldn't maintain the darkness. He felt it disintegrate and break off into small pieces. He struggled to hold it together. Something struck him in the side of the face.

He looked up from the floor to see Doc Stone standing over him.

"I'll give you an 'A' for effort," the school counselor taunted. "That was an impressive ability. You've got potential. Maybe the Liberator can use you."

With the darkness dispelled, Rusty's light dominated the room. The glare made everything look as if a coat of white paint had been splashed everywhere. Over by the boarded-up picture window, Damon spied Denise and Vee, blinded and confused. They would be of no help.

Damon heard a door open from somewhere and footsteps approaching. He strained to see the figure, covered head to toe in a Mexican blanket.

Chapter Twelve
The Gang's All Here

Thoughts flooded Damon's mind. *What is Kierra doing here? Why is she so casually walking into Calvin's house?* He felt sick to realize that Eddie may not be the only traitor in the Secret Club.

The figure pulled the Mexican blanket tight across herself as she strode past Calvin and the open rift. Calvin, still struggling to close the rift, followed the figure with his eyes but had to avert his gaze because of Rusty's glare.

"Who th' hell?"

The figure ignored Calvin and walked straight up to Rusty.

"You must be Rusty," she said in a tittering voice.

Rusty seemed taken aback that a girl—even one he couldn't see—had called him by name. "Yeah. Who're you?"

Now that she was closer, Damon could see she held the blanket up to her face, covering most of it, except for large, dark glasses.

"Damon told me about you, so I know all about your power." She tried to sound confident, even cocky. "If you don't turn it off, you'll regret it!"

Rusty, whom Damon could still see only as an outline within the glare, turned to face her. "Oh, so you're with Damon, huh? Well, it was really stupid of you to come here." He reached out a hand toward her, and Damon jumped. Rusty intended to murder her, right in front of his eyes!

Kierra threw back the blanket, as if she were expecting, even wanting this. The glare from Rusty intensified.

"Everyone!" Damon shouted. "Shield your eyes!"

Damon exhaled, creating a dark space that surrounded himself, Rusty and Kierra, but the two, locked in their impending battle, didn't seem to notice. A ray of sunlight shot from Rusty's hand and struck Kierra, enveloping her. But the girl held her ground, stretched out her arms as if she were bathing in the energy and then, fists clenched, thrust her arms together. The solar energy shot back to its source.

The glare was so intense that, even in the dark space, Damon had to shut his eyes.

Rusty screamed. "My eyes!"

"It's okay, Damon," Kierra called. "You can make the dark space go away."

Damon inhaled and opened his eyes, taking in a sight he had seen before, but it was never quite so beautiful. Kierra stood before him in her crystalline form, light refracting across the room as if it were daylight. She smiled at him. "You were right. My power does counteract his."

"What the hell's goin' on?" Calvin yelled. The distraction had caused him to lose control of the rift. Danner pushed it wider. He had shrunk to a size of eight feet so he could easily crawl through it and into the room. Calvin skittered away from the hulking, bleeding giant before him. "Doc!"

Damon had forgotten about Doc Stone. He turned around, but the man wasn't there. He heard the door open again from around the corner in the living room, followed by a growl. It was the deep, inhuman growl of a large dog. *Or a werewolf.*

There were sounds of a scuffle around the corner. They continued even after the werewolf appeared in view. Covered head to toe in fur, Eddie stood on all fours and opened his maw, bearing fangs. His growl reverberated across the room, announcing to everyone that no one would get past him.

By the picture window, Vee started to blur. Denise grabbed his shoulder and shook her head.

Great! Damon thought. *The one guy who could get away or do something, and you're afraid for his safety.* Damon stared at the wolf and felt no fear, only hatred. *I brought you into this club, so I'll deal with you— traitor!*

The wolf leaped past Damon and landed on Calvin.

Damon spun around and nearly lost his balance. A rift had opened behind him—a rift that led to a dimension of jagged rocks. It shut quickly, now that Calvin was too busy to maintain it.

"Get off me! Get off me!" Calvin screamed as he wrestled on the floor with the werewolf.

Damon stared, processing the reality that Eddie had just saved his life. "Eddie's with us?"

"Things aren't what you think they are," said Kierra with a radiant crystalline smile. She ran over to assist Sami.

The scuffle around the corner ended with a SMACK! Doc Stone stumbled into view and collapsed. Gareth rounded the corner, his body puffed up into super-strong muscles. His attention zeroed in on the ceiling, and his face twisted into revulsion and determination. "Hey, Perv! You're mine."

Now that he was free, Damon could see Ali dangling from the ceiling, her arms above her, wrapped in the black gunk that extended its way into the ceiling. A pair of sinister eyes opened in the gunk.

"Gareth Sanderson, is it?" a deep voice came from within the gunk. "Well, well, I haven't seen you since the old Forbidden Neighborhood. Your brother and I were close friends, you know. *Very* close."

"Don't talk about my brother!" Gareth shouted. "Come down here and face me!"

"I think not," the gunk replied. "So long as I've got this pretty girl here, I'm safe from you, from all of you." The gunk tightened its grip on Ali's arms. She cried out.

Damon joined Gareth and Danner as they formed an arc around Ali. Despite his wounds, Danner remained at eight feet, just a foot below the ceiling. He reached up and clawed at the gunk.

"Back!" Old Lie roared. "Or I'll break her arms!"

Damon prepared to exhale. A well-timed dark force could take Old Lie by surprise, causing him to lose his grip on Ali. Or it could cause him to snap her arms. He looked back and forth at Gareth and Danner, hoping they had a better idea.

"Now, this is how it's going to be," Old Lie said through an unseen mouth. "I'm going to come down from the ceiling and encase myself around your friend here. Then the two of us are going to walk out of here.

Got it?"

No one budged.

"GOT IT?" Old Lie repeated. The gunk hardened around Ali's arms. Her face turned blue from the loss of circulation.

She opened her eyes, a look of raw determination. "You're not touching me any further!" She began swinging back and forth.

Old Lie had no visible mouth, but the large, oblong eyes narrowed as if their owner was grinning. "You're not going to shake yourself loose from me, girl. You're mine, now!"

Ali swung faster. "Who...says...I'm...trying...to ...shake loose?" In one swift move, she defied gravity and swung her feet up into the eyes.

The unseen mouth screamed, and the gunk spread in every direction, losing cohesion. Ali fell into Danner's arms.

Gareth grabbed a piece of gunk that fell within reach and yanked it, pulling Old Lie loose from the ceiling. The gunk reassembled itself into something resembling a human being. To Damon, it looked not like the boy he had seen in the restroom or even someone in his early 20s, but a withered old man. It struggled to reshape itself into a bear. Gareth swung the ridiculous shape around and smashed it into the wall.

Damon jumped back and forth, trying to find some way to help.

"Damon!" Denise called. "You have to go after Calvin! Now!"

"But he's right—" Damon looked around the room.

Calvin and the werewolf were gone.

Chapter Thirteen
Showdown

Damon didn't want to go after Calvin by himself. He was tired and hungry from the long journey up the hill in the other dimension. And, if he had to face Calvin, why couldn't Vee and Denise go with him?

Vee had taken the rope used to tie Sami up and hog-tied Doc Stone while the latter was still unconscious. Denise told her brother to search the house for medical supplies to help with Danner's injuries and with Ali, who was dazed from the fall. She reminded Damon that they still needed to find Jayden. Kierra couldn't come—with her crystalline form reflecting light, she might as well announce they were coming. And Sami refused. "Super-hearing, not useful in battle?" she reminded Damon.

Damon had no idea where to even search. Denise told him to go outside—the front.

So, Damon found himself outside staring from the top of the steps, looking for some sign of Calvin and Eddie. The neighborhood was dark, except for the streetlights. The houses were older and larger, just like Calvin's. Many were run-down, and most of the lawns were not well-kept. It was a dismal and depressing area to look at. Damon wondered if the neighbors had heard the fight inside Calvin's supposedly vacant house. Didn't matter. They wouldn't call the police. It was standard operating procedure to let powered kids do what they wanted in the district. *Like being overrun by a gang.*

He turned to go back inside and report that he couldn't find Calvin when he heard a noise from across the street. It sounded like an animal crying out in pain.

Every fiber in Damon's body resisted as he leapt down the stairs and ran across the street. The Power Club was an unbeatable team. Damon felt lost without them. *What if I make it worse? What if I screw up?*

The animal cried out again. This time it sounded half human. *Eddie.*

The direction of the scream led Damon into a backyard. Concealed by a row of bushes, he looked down the alley and saw Calvin standing between two garages. Calvin waved his hand in the air and appeared to be concentrating.

A rift opened above him, and a half-wolf Eddie tumbled out of a dimension that glowed red and yellow. Eddie flopped around on the gravel. His fur was singed.

"You got p'tential, Costa," Calvin gloated. "Swear allegiance t' the Liberator, an' I'll let you stay."

Damon stepped into the alley. "Hey, Calvin! Let Eddie go. It's me you want."

Calvin's coal-black eyes narrowed as he looked up. "Where's your widdle friends, Damon? Did you come here by yourself? Tha' was stupid!" He gestured toward Damon.

Damon jumped back behind the bushes. No rift appeared.

"Ha! Ha! Ha! You coward!" Calvin roared. "You don' even matter anymore. So you busted up our ring. Big deal. Me an' the Liberator got more warriors back at th' compound! We're gonna start a war, an' the first thing I'm gonna do is come back here and sen' your family away. I'll send 'em to a gas giant or a worl' made of lava, or..."

Damon crouched and ran down the side of the yard. Facing Calvin head on would be too dangerous. He would have to sneak up behind him.

The hedges concealing Damon vanished into a rift that opened underneath them. Damon ran behind some more hedges. They, too, vanished.

"C'me out, c'me out, wherever you are!" Calvin taunted. "All ye in come...dead!"

Damon's path was blocked by a garage. He turned to see Calvin enter the yard where the row of hedges had been.

"I jus' thought of somethin'. First time you fough' me, it was in an alley. Now, here we are in an alley again. Kinda fitting, don' you think?" He took a step to the left. "Only this time, I'm not getting close enough for you to use your dark space. I don' need t' get that close t' sen' you away for good!"

The ground below Damon's feet gave way. In desperation, he turned to the garage and latched onto a ladder affixed to the side. Noxious fumes resembling ammonia and wax assaulted him from below. He refused to look down.

He dangled for what seemed like an eternity. *Why doesn't Calvin just send the entire garage into the rift?* Then he remembered something Jayden had said. Damon hooked his arm around the rungs and held onto the side of the ladder with the tightest grip he could make.

"What's the matter, Calvin?" he shouted. "Losing your touch?"

"Wha's tha' s'pposed to mean?"

"Jayden told us what the Liberator feeds you, how it weakens powers and you have to keep taking the antidote so you don't lose your powers."

"Tha's for th' other kids! Tha's not for me!"

"Are you sure?" Damon looked over his shoulder. Calvin wore the most confident, most evil expression he had ever seen. "Then how come you couldn't close the rift while Danner was inside it? How come you work harder to create rifts than you used to?"

"Tha's a lie!" Calvin bellowed.

Damon grinned. "Then how come I'm still here?"

Calvin frothed with rage. "I'll show you!" He stepped forward and concentrated. The rift below Damon widened. The garage teetered.

Damon pretended to yawn. "Is that the best you can do?"

"YOU!" Calvin charged toward Damon.

Close enough! Damon reached around with his free hand, pointed to Calvin and exhaled. A bolt of dark force shot out and wrapped itself around Calvin's torso. Damon yanked the dark force toward him like a lasso.

"NO!" Calvin screamed as the rift loomed before him. His eyes narrowed, and he puffed up his cheeks to concentrate. But the rift did not change. "It's no' working! I can' close it!"

"The Liberator betrayed you, Calvin! You're losing your power. You're becoming an ord—just like the people he wants to kill!"

Calvin looked Damon in the eye, but instead of seeing an evil being

156

who wanted to send other people away for good, who wanted to kill ords, Damon saw only a kid—a frightened, lonely kid who never grew up beyond the second grade.

What happened next Damon couldn't be sure. Calvin tripped or jumped. Or perhaps Damon yanked a little too hard. He wanted to bring Calvin closer to the rift, to show him that if he fell in, Calvin would fall in, too. But Calvin fell in, alone. The rift sealed behind him.

Damon released his grip on the ladder and collapsed onto grass and dirt. He waited to see if Calvin would reappear.

A noise startled him. It took him a moment to identify it. He had heard the *whup-whup-whup* before only on television. He craned his neck to see a helicopter passing above the trees, its searchlight cutting a white-blue swath through the darkness. On the chopper's underbelly, Damon spied the call-letters of a news station from the city.

~ * ~

Damon found Eddie where he'd fallen in the middle of the alley. Damon approached with caution, both out of concern for this guy who had so recently become his friend and because he still wasn't sure whose side Eddie was on.

Denise's visions had been accurate all along. All except one. The one of the monster next to Calvin.

Eddie looked up as Damon approached. "Hey, D," he said with a grin. He was clad only in grey sweatpants Damon had seen him wear at Eddie's house.

"Hey, E..." Damon couldn't say his name. Not then and there. He had to know. "So, you weren't on Calvin's side?"

Eddie looked as if he'd been hurt. "What? No! Sami told me what you said, why you didn't call me. I was working with the district all along. They wanted me to keep an eye on you."

"Why?"

"'Cause you're special, Damon. You can get people to work with you and do things. They knew if you learned Calvin was back, you'd go after him."

Damon smiled at the irony of it all. "Why didn't they stop me?"

"Because they couldn't find Calvin. They knew you'd expose him, get him out in the open. See, this is a lot bigger than you and Calvin. They didn't know about Doc Stone. They didn't know he was recruiting kids for the Liberator."

Damon felt an emotion he hadn't felt before. It wasn't pride, exactly. He had been used, used by the district and even by Eddie. But this was a lot bigger than that. A terrorist was going around murdering people. A terrorist who wanted to start a war. Damon was connected to all that, whether he wanted to be or not—and tonight he had made a difference. He had heard adults talk about feeling humbled before. He had always thought it sounded silly. Now, he figured he knew what they meant.

All that mattered to him, for the moment, was that he had gotten his friends back home, and his other friends had come to rescue them. And Eddie was a friend. At least for now.

Damon extended a hand. "Do you need help?"

Eddie grabbed the hand. "I think I wrenched my paw when I landed in the alley." He held his left leg as Damon pulled him up.

Damon helped him hobble through the yard and back to the street. Blue and white police lights flashed across the area. Damon hadn't even heard the sirens.

"Standard procedure," Eddie said through the pain of his twisted ankle. "When they launch a major operation like this, they don't want people to know they're coming."

"Major operation?" Damon had heard the term used for drug busts in the city, not with things happening in the district—where the worst that could happen consisted of some powered kid destroying a car or house. *Or sending other kids away.* Several police cars and ambulances blocked the street in front of Calvin's house. Officers climbed the steps and entered the house.

In the back of one of the police cars Damon saw a familiar face. It was Jayden. Spotting Damon, he leaned through the open window and waved.

"Hey, Damon!"

Damon led Eddie up to the car.

"I'm glad you made it!" Jayden shouted. "When I came back, I got away from Calvin and the others. Then I went to the police station and told them what was going on."

"But how did you get to the police station?"

Jayden pointed to the phone lines criss-crossing the neighborhood. "You should've seen the desk sergeant when he picked up the phone and I jumped out. I thought he was going to have an accident." Jayden covered his mouth as he laughed.

Damon could only shake his head. After all this, Jayden—who had just saved all of their lives—was just a kid who laughed at pee and poop jokes.

The bright light of the news chopper passed over Damon, Eddie, and Jayden and illuminated the house as two officers led Doc Stone out in bulbous nullcuffs that negated his power.

"What's the news doing here?" Eddie scowled at the chopper. "How'd they even know about this?"

Damon smiled. Miss Vogel had come through, after all. The district wouldn't be able to keep this a secret. Not anymore.

A minivan pulled up to the end of the block, where the police cars had blocked traffic. As the headlights shut off, the front doors opened and out jumped Mr. and Mrs. Evans. They stopped and talked to one of the officers.

The back doors of the minivan opened, and out jumped Damon's mother and brother. In that moment, he lost it. Eddie was busy chatting with Jayden, so Damon left him leaning against the police car and walked toward the minivan. When Eldon spotted Damon and pointed to him, the walk turned into a trot and then a run. Damon couldn't hear anything. All he saw was his mother and brother running toward him. He fell into her arms and sobbed.

He got what he wanted all along. He got his family back.

Epilogue

Barney loads the vans. I put Celia in charge of the children. With her web powers, she ought to keep them in line. Longtrees has gone ahead to make sure the roads are safe.

We lost today.

We lost Brothers Stone and Viouet. Even the Reddick boy was captured. Now we must abandon the Pacific compound, the only home most of us have ever known.

Too soon. Too soon to involve children in our war. They are not ready. They were defeated by more children.

Aerial footage from the scene floods social media. The house where we held our base of operations right in the heart of the district. The maps used to plan our next strike. The faces of our lost brothers.

But we are not the only ones who lost. The district lost its veil of secrecy over the powered children forced to live in its boundaries. While the names of the children involved have been kept out of the media, it is known that children stopped the "terrorist" threat, as they call us. It is known that children made a difference. Some even call for restrictions on the Powered to be lifted.

Let them have their heroes. Let them have their day.

My phone buzzes. The hidden network. I do not answer. He is no longer one of us and he will not return. The null enzymes we fed him were stronger than most, my insurance that he would never turn against us.

Besides, with the transdimensonal network, we have what we need from him.

Goodbye, Calvin. You let your personal hatred for one boy get the best of you. You cost us.

You didn't learn to use your hatred, to reign it in, to control it, as I have controlled mine. The district will fail. Ords will die. And the Neumeyer boy will lead the way.

Prologue
A Special Club

A brown-and-white police car pulled up to Damon's house. Damon sat in the back on a dull leather seat which reeked of sweat and vomit—not his own. Tears burned his cheeks as he held his breath, trying not to retch. He couldn't believe someone called the cops. He couldn't believe they arrested him instead of the kids who stole his bike.

"Arrested" wasn't the right word. The cops didn't put handcuffs on him. Still, the two officers kept their null-guns and shock batons ready. Damon felt like a criminal.

The officers let Damon out in front of his house for all the neighbors to see. He wanted to hide from prying eyes—but he knew using his power again would get him in more trouble. To drive home this point, the police warned his mother, when they escorted him to the front door, that Damon must never use his power in public again.

"Don't worry about the bike." Damon's mother cleaned his lip where the winged boy split it before the cops showed up. "Your father and I will buy you a new one next spring."

"Mom," he said, exasperated, "I don't want a new bike. Call the police chief. Maybe he'll send some officers to get my bike back."

"Honey, that's not how things work in the district."

Ow! Damon's lip stung as his mom dabbed it with a damp cloth. She held his arm tight as he tried to squirm away.

"What were you doing in that neighborhood?" she said. "It's in a dangerous part of the district. You know you're not supposed to go there."

Damon blubbered, "I dunno." His mother wouldn't understand. He had lived in the district almost as long as he could remember, but there were parts of it he had never seen and wanted to explore—even though the district was very small, only about two and a half miles long. He couldn't leave the district without permission from the government and wasn't even allowed to use his power except at home or school. This rule, he'd just found out, applied even to self-defense.

The incident burned in his memory. When he rode up the hill, he saw two powered kids out playing. One boy sprouted bat-like wings and flew over the other kid, who reached out to him with puffy, mist-enshrouded arms which resembled clouds. These kids were using their powers freely. *Maybe*, Damon thought, *the rules did not apply in their neighborhood.*

But when Damon tried to join in on the fun, they jeered at him: "You don't belong to our special club." The cloud boy reached out with his arms, the force blowing Damon off his bike. Then the batwing boy swooped down and made a play for the bike. "We'll just keep your bike for trespassing in our neighborhood."

Damon did the only thing he could do, the only thing he'd been trained to do. He exhaled, and the darkness came. His dark-space, as he called it, was just a field of darkness. Sometimes, depending on his mood, it resembled a cloud. Other times, it appeared as a void. Damon could make it large enough to fill a room, if he wanted. No one inside the dark-space could see, except for him. People and objects appeared black and white in his night vision, the term he preferred. No one could hear, either, unless he opened a sound-space.

The void of darkness had the desired effect. It frightened the kids, who suddenly couldn't see or hear. Damon should have pedaled away, he now realized. Instead he reached forward and extended his thumb and forefinger, opening a sound-space so he could tell them he didn't mean to trespass and only wanted to play with them. Big mistake. The kids followed the sound of his voice and ganged up on him. Damon got away. Then the cops came.

"What did those kids mean," he asked his mother, "about belonging to a special club?"

Leah Neumeyer folded the damp cloth and put it aside. She sat on the ottoman—Damon lounged in the recliner—and looked at the floor of the living room. "Well, I guess you were going to learn about them sooner or later. The district allows older kids to use their powers in public if they belong to certain kinds of clubs. The clubs have to be registered with the district, and they have to follow rules."

"Like being allowed to steal other kids' bikes?"

"Oh, hush, honey. A lot of things in the district aren't fair. Remember when we first moved here and your dad's car got stolen?"

Damon nodded.

"Well, it wasn't really stolen. Some boy who could bend metal destroyed it. The district gave your dad a new car, but they made us promise not to tell anyone what really happened."

Damon remembered. The new car was smaller and didn't have electric windows.

"But why does the district let kids form special clubs?"

"No one really knows," his mother answered. She leaned closer, as if she were expecting someone to listen in. "They say kids learn to use their powers better by working together. But some people think it's so they can see what you kids can really do."

"But why would they want to know?"

His mother seemed uncomfortable with the question. "Honey, it's been a long time since we moved to the district. Have you forgotten ordinary people such as your dad, me, or Eldon—"

"Ords?"

"Honey, I told you, that's not a nice word."

"Sorry," he said, biting his lip.

"Anyway, ordinary people are sometimes afraid of kids with powers."

Her explanation made Damon remember why he and his family

were forced to move to the district in the first place. Just after his sixth birthday, he discovered he could create darkness just by thinking about it and exhaling. His mother told him to keep his ability a secret, but Damon couldn't wait to share it with his friends in the neighborhood. They loved it. They would run into the black cloud and scream with delight.

Then Ryan, a snotty kid who lived up the street, joined in. He came to Damon's tiny backyard and told Damon to create a dark-space just for him. Damon obliged. If he could impress Ryan, he thought, they could be friends. But as the darkness approached him, Ryan panicked and ran into the alley. A car screeched to a halt inches in front of him.

It was Ryan's parents who ratted Damon out to the city council. He still recalled how he felt when his parents told him they would have to move to the district. It wasn't far, but to Damon, it might as well have been the North Pole.

The memory stung like an open wound. "People're afraid of me? That's stupid."

"It is stupid, honey," his mother said. "But we live in a stupid world. No one knows why some kids develop powers and others don't. Your brother, for example—"

Damon tuned her out. He was tired of his mother reminding him how Eldon demonstrated no special abilities. He hated it when she pointed out how "ordinary" his kid brother was. Damon felt he was being punished for having a power.

He waited for her to finish. "Mom, I want to join a club."

Her eyes flashed. "There aren't any special clubs in this neighborhood."

"Then I'll start one."

"You're too young. I think you have to be at least twelve and a half."

Damon banged the arm of the recliner. His twelfth birthday was still four months away. "Why twelve and a half? Why not twelve?" he demanded to know.

"A lot of the district's rules don't make sense. Just forget about the special clubs. Now, when your dad comes home, he's going to expect the yard to be mowed, which you should have done before you took off."

"Okay," Damon muttered. "After I mow the lawn, can I help Dad in the garage?"

His mother looked askance, reminding Damon of the last time he helped his father restore furniture. Bored, Damon created a dark-space just for fun. This prompted his dad to lecture him on how dangerous a drill and saw could be and to banish his firstborn son from the garage. Damon was hurt. His father worked for the district and restored furniture as a hobby. It was almost the only time Damon got to spend with him.

"I'll talk to your father," his mother said with a sense of relief. Damon imagined how the conversation would go: "Now, Ray, if you let Damon work with you in the garage, like a father should, he'll forget all about these special clubs." Ray Neumeyer would capitulate, as he always did.

But his mother was wrong. Damon would never forget about the special clubs. They could help him do something his father couldn't: teach him how to use his power. Sooner or later, someone in his neighborhood would start a special club, and, when they did, Damon promised himself he would be the first to join.

Chapter One
Try Out

"IS THAT THE BEST YOU CAN DO?" shouted Veryl Evans. He raced past Damon.

"That's not fair!" Damon shouted back. "Hold still!"

Veryl—Vee, as he preferred—ran circles around Damon, easily evading the dark-space. His voice seemed to come from everywhere. "If we were criminals, we wouldn't hold still."

Damon strained to make the darkness come faster, but the gentle cloud flowed slowly from every pore in his body. *Why couldn't I have a cool power, one that moves faster?* By the time the darkness spread ten feet, Vee was long gone.

Damon inhaled to make the dark-space go away and glowered. Vee, nearly a year younger, was already a member of a special club. Damon, four months past his thirteenth birthday, had failed to keep his promise. He was not the first to join. But he would be the next.

He turned to face his next opponent, Danner ("Don't call me Danny.") Young. The fourteen-year-old showed off his power by remaining at six feet almost always, but, no matter how tall he could grow, Damon would make sure it wasn't tall enough.

Damon closed his eyes and inhaled, envisioning a void of darkness shooting straight up. But Danner didn't appear worried. He flexed his muscles and started to grow: ten feet...fifteen...twenty. Then the older kid's head disappeared! *Oh. He's just grown too big for the dark-space.* Damon struggled to make the void stretch, but could only watch as Danner's torso and legs turned and strode out of the darkness.

"HEY, DAMON," someone close to him shouted. "THIS DARKNESS IS A NEAT TRICK."

Damon turned to face his third opponent, Kyle Powell. At fifteen, Kyle was the oldest member of the Power Club and the most powerful. Yet there he stood; deaf and blind. Feeling powerful, Damon opened a sound-space.

"Hey, Kyle, why are you just standing there looking stupid?"

If the comment irked Kyle, he didn't show. "I don't teleport when I can't see where I'm going. Might merge with a tree or something."

Perfect. If Damon could defeat Kyle, he'd be in the Power Club for sure.

"So, is this it?" Kyle said, looking around at nothing. "Can your darkness do anything else?"

It doesn't have to. Damon carefully closed the sound-space so Kyle wouldn't hear him. Then he ran toward Kyle. *All I have to do is trip him.* A feeling of immense power overcame him as he approached the unsuspecting kid, then—

...*fft.*

Damon found himself floating. He couldn't sense anything. He felt as if his body were liquid, being scrambled and rearranged. His head lay on his torso. Now it jutted from under his left knee. His thumb protruded from the opposite side of his hand.

Normal sensation gradually returned. Blue sky...hot summer air...birds chirping...and Damon found himself standing in midair. He dropped three feet to the ground, landed on his feet, and fell to his back. The park spun, and he felt sick.

He forced himself to sit up and saw a huge, twenty-foot, black cloud floating above where he'd been standing. It was his dark-space. *Awesome!*

The black cloud lingered. Then, slowly, it turned grey and vanished, leaving behind its sole occupant, Kyle Powell.

Kyle jogged over to Damon.

"I thought you said you couldn't teleport when you can't see where you're going!" Damon scolded him.

"I said I don't teleport." A sly grin came to Kyle's lips. "But I keep my teleporter field on, just in case."

"But you could've—" Sensation returned to his legs. Damon struggled to stand and talk at the same time. "You could've teleported me into a tree."

"Nah. I know Mack Park pretty well. I just needed to make sure you were a few feet off the ground."

Vee and Danner, who shrunk back to six feet, joined them. "You musta tried to attack Kyle, didn't ya?" Danner teased. "Don't feel too bad. I used to do the same thing."

"Yeah, but you tried to sneak up on me more than once," Kyle responded. "Maybe Damon's smart and will learn his lesson the first time."

They bantered back and forth, but Damon felt both in and out of the group. Growing impatient, he asked, "So, what happens next?"

"Now," Vee answered, "we vote."

"In private," Kyle added.

Damon took the hint and jogged several feet away toward the sandpit where a group of younger kids played on a slide. He snuck a glance back once or twice to see the three Power Club members huddling. When he glanced back a third time, Kyle was running toward him—alone.

Damon steeled himself.

"Your power's okay," Kyle began, "but it's not strong enough for the Power Club. You need more practice."